ALPHA'S MISSION

A SPECIAL FORCES SHIFTER ROMANCE

RENEE ROSE

LEE SAVINO

BURNING DESIRES

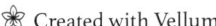 Created with Vellum

ALPHA'S MISSION

THE MONSTER WANTS HER. HE WON'T BE DENIED.

I've become a monster.

I hear blood moving in people's veins. Scent their emotions.

I want to feed. To hunt. To mate...

I'm no longer a human—my life is over.

I've left everyone I love. I've gone rogue from the CIA.

My only hope is my handler.

Annabel Gray is tough enough to face my monster. If I lose control, she won't hesitate to take me out. But I'm not the only predator out there. Someone's hunting Annabel.

She needs my protection.

But if I don't get my animal under control,

I may be her biggest threat yet.

PROLOGUE

Appalachian Mountains, Kentucky
Full Moon, 1993

Charlie

A COYOTE HOWLS and the hair of the back of my neck stands up. My grandparent's cabin creaks in the wind. I'm spending the night with them like I always do on weekends when my mom is in town tending bar.

"If I didn't know better, I'd say that's a wolf," Grandma says, dusting flour off her hands. "But Kentucky hasn't seen wolves in over a hundred years."

"I've seen a wolf." The moment I say it, I wish I hadn't although I can't understand the twisting in my gut. All I know is that huge silver wolf—the one I've come to think of as mine, the one I often feel watching me—doesn't want to be talked about.

My uncle snorts.

My grandfather looks at me sharply. "Where'd you see a wolf, boy?"

Now I really wish I hadn't said anything. I shake my head. "Nowhere."

My grandfather gets up from his chair, brows down. "Don't lie. You said you saw a wolf. Was it big and gray?"

I swallow and nod.

"Somethin' unnatural about it? Somethin' strange? Like it was *too* big for a wolf?

Again, I nod.

A howl sounds again, this time closer. My grandfather picks up his shotgun from behind the door. My two uncles get up and do the same.

"Harold, no," my grandmother cries.

My grandfather ignores her and opens the door to our cabin, stepping outside into the moonlight. "It's time we take these woods back," he says, rough determination in the set of his shoulders.

I scramble up to follow them, picking up the BB gun he's already taught me how to use and following them out. Grandpa always lets me go with him—I'm pretty much his shadow when I'm at his place, so I'm surprised when he turns and holds up a hand.

"No. You can't come this time, Charlie. Get in the house and protect your grandma."

My shoulders draw back at the directive *protect your grandma,* and I run back inside to sit by the window with the BB gun across my lap.

I don't know how much time passes before I hear a shot not far from the cabin. I leap to my feet and run to the back door, the direction it came from, throwing open the door.

"Charlie, don't come out here," my grandfather warns in

a low voice. He's twenty feet away, standing with his back to me. My uncles stand beside him, blocking my view of whatever they're looking at on the ground. There's something in his voice that frightens me—like *he's* afraid. But that doesn't make sense, he's never afraid.

"Did you get it, Grandpa?"

"Yeah, I got somethin' all right." Again, he sounds strange. "You get in the house and tell your grandma to call Devon." Devon is Grandpa's brother who lives on the property next door. I relay the message and position myself in the open door. Grandma crowds up behind me, but there's nothing to see. Grandpa's already dragging something away from the cabin through the woods. I start to go out, but Grandma catches my shoulder.

"If your grandpa told you to stay in the house, you need to stay put."

I reluctantly let her lead me back inside and shut the door. She turns the television on for me, but I have no interest. I stay at the windows, watching Grandpa and my uncles moving about, talking. I slide the window open to listen.

"It *was* a wolf. The big gray one—the one Callie saw when she was a teen," my grandpa says.

Callie's my mom. I have a daddy, but he doesn't come around much. He comes by on my birthday, brings me gifts, but she won't let him come in, never lets him take me anywhere. She seems afraid of him although I've never seen any reason for it.

"Well he ain't a wolf now, Harold," Devon says. There's doubt dripping in his words like he doesn't believe what my Grandpa saw. "You know who that is, don't you?"

Who, not *what.*

"I know."

A chill runs through me. Did my grandpa kill a man?

Will he go to jail?

"Go get the shovels," my grandpa says to my uncles. "We'll have to bury it out here on the property."

"Come away from there, Charlie." My grandma slams the window shut. "It's long past your bedtime. Go brush your teeth." I hear fear in her voice, too, which is why I don't argue. I put the gun up and go to bed.

It will take years for me to realize my father's disappearance from my life coincided with that night.

1

C *harlie*

BLOOD IN MY MOUTH... not mine.

Tastes... so good.

No. Not good. Wrong.

Change back, dammit.

Shift.

When nothing happens, I tear up the mountainside, through the trees, leaping over fallen logs and boulders. My white paws are huge on the soft pine needles.

What's that? Movement in the bushes. I leap and twist in the air, take off after the running jackrabbit.

It doesn't stand a chance. I'm too fast. Too ferocious.

More blood fills my mouth, hot and thick. I gobble down the rabbit's flesh like a starved dog.

Then I trot down to the creek and drink from it.

When I see my reflection in the water, I bite at the big, silver and white wolf.

Shift, you monster. Shift.

I don't even know where the fuck I am. How to get back. My brain doesn't work right. I have no control over my body. My... urges.

I turn and trot in the direction I'm pulled and somehow, miraculously, end up in front of my truck.

The desire to get in that truck and drive off this mountain, away from what happened here is so strong, I sit and whine at the door handle.

Shift back.

What did Jared say to make me change back in Honduras? Just *shift back*. I cast my mind to that moment, seeing my white paws for the first time, the heat and rearranging of my cells, and suddenly, I'm on my side, naked, panting.

Human.

Thank fuck.

I'm human again. Eighteen hours I've been roaming this mountain trying to figure out how to change back.

Coming here and letting the monster out was a mistake. I wipe my mouth, disgusted by the taste of blood. When the memory of what I ate comes flooding back, I heave behind the car.

Christ. It's not like me to not have my own body under control. This sack of bones has been a machine for me from the moment I entered the Army and got out of Kentucky at age eighteen. I can kill with my bare hands, escape any danger. I work best under pressure.

This is no time to get sensitive.

I just can't stand feeling out of control, not knowing what I'm going to do next. The way I succumbed to the animal's need to hunt—I couldn't control it. The way the waxing moon brought me out here last night.

Shit. What time is it?

I grab the keys I hid on top of the driver's side wheel and open the truck.

Twelve-fucking-thirty. I missed a meeting with my handler. I'm so fucked.

I yank on my jeans while I call Agent Annabel Gray.

"Dune, what happened to you? You've been off the grid for twenty hours." She'd checked my tracking device. I only keep it on when I'm on an active mission.

Do I hear relief in her voice? Was Ann Gray worried about me? It's an odd thought, but my relationship with her changed last month when I asked her for help tracking the... *werewolves*. Now, I know what they are.

What *I* am.

Anyway, there's trust between us. She did me a favor, said I owe her one in return.

That piece of information has had me mulling over what I know about her. What could she possibly need from me?

"I'm sorry," I say, pulling on my shirt and getting behind the wheel. "I missed our meeting."

"Is everything okay?" There's an awkward hesitation in her voice. It *is* personal.

"I'm not hurt." That much is true. For some reason, I don't want to lie to her, and I'm definitely not okay.

Finding out I'm a werewolf—having my werewolf genes triggered or activated by seeing others of... my kind —definitely threw me for a loop. I question my sanity on a daily basis. But more importantly, I question my efficacy. My senses are in overdrive. I hear too much, smell too many scents, crave meat like I'm going to die if I don't kill something. If I can't control my animalistic urges, what's going to happen when I'm on a job? When lives are at risk?

"I spent the night... out of the city. I can meet in ninety minutes. Give me a location."

She blows out an impatient breath. "Venice Beach, 1430 hours."

"I'll find you there."

I hang up my phone and step on the gas. I don't usually give a shit about pissed off handlers. My job performance isn't graded on how well I interface with others, it's how well I complete my missions. But for some reason—maybe because she sounded like she cared—I'm in a hurry to see Agent Gray face to face.

Maybe even to apologize.

Annabel

I BUY an ice cream cone and sit on the wall at Venice Beach, blending in with the hordes of beachgoers. I dressed to fit in —I'm wearing a halter top and shorts with wrap-around sandals I can run in if I need to.

I can't believe I'm upset Charlie Dune hooked up with someone last night. Why in the hell would I care?

We don't have a relationship.

I'm his handler, for God's sake.

Yeah, he's hot. All the field agents I've met appeal to me. I mean what's not enthralling about highly intelligent men whose bodies are trained weapons? Agents who supposedly can single-handedly bring down governments or start wars? Agents who can rescue hostages or—rumor has it—execute a kill order? I know I've never passed along orders like that, but my clearance level isn't high.

Dune, like all field agents, is built of chiseled muscle. He's not huge or tall, they never are. They need to be able to slip in and out of places unnoticed—blend in.

I have a thing for spies, I guess, particularly Dune. Something happened last month between us. Actually, it's probably all in my head. Which is why I'm an intelligence analyst, not a field agent—I over-emotionalize, get personal with people and situations. I care too deeply. Despite my basic combat training, I'd never be able to pull the trigger on anyone even if my life depended on it.

I bent some rules and put my own job on the line to get some information last month for Dune. He said he lost someone involved with the lab fires. And I probably over-personalized that. Because I know what it's like to investigate our government's dirty secrets when it involves a loved one.

"Chocolate—my favorite," a deep voice rumbles behind me.

I don't jump. I'm used to him appearing out of thin air. What I'm not used to is how close he comes in. If I didn't think it was crazy, I'd swear he leaned in to inhale my scent.

I turn and find his face too near to mine, and the green of his eyes appears to change to ice blue in the sunlight.

Damn.

Yeah, he's hotter than I remembered. In a tight black t-shirt—the kind that stretches over his hard muscles—and a ball cap pulled low over his green eyes, he looks the perfect hunky, California surfer.

He steals the ice cream cone from me and takes a big lick. Well, this is definitely different. We're practically sharing spit.

Is he flirting?

Oh, that's ripe. After he missed our morning meeting because of some hook-up he had. I never knew Dune was such a player, but it fits. Field agents can't have permanent relationships, so they become man-whores, getting it whenever and wherever they want.

Asshole.

I turn to face him and watch as he completely demolishes the ice cream cone. I mean, I didn't know you could eat a cone that fast.

So, I guess we're not sharing spit.

He has the grace to look shame-faced as he licks the last bit off his fingers.

"I'll buy you another one."

I roll my eyes. "Don't bother. I only bought it for cover."

"What's the assignment?"

I can't stop my annoyance from surfacing even though he's always all-business.

"Your no-show this morning may have cost us the mission."

His face remains impassive, and under the ballcap, his eyes keep roving the landscape like he's taking in every person who passes, everything about our surroundings. He's so damn *alert*.

"I'll fix it. What's the mission?"

The thing is—I believe him. I'm sure he'll fix it. He's the kind of agent who gets results which is why he gets paid the big bucks.

Still, I'm not over feeling pissy. I flick on my tablet and share the screen with him. "Target is Lucius Frangelico. He lives in Hollywood. Occupation, unknown. Possible mafia, possible drug kingpin. Definitely into something. They want him bugged and tracked."

"Why is this a CIA job rather than FBI?"

"He has ties to Al Qaeda. Travels internationally. May be selling weaponry. This is a preliminary investigation."

"I'll take care of it."

"Yeah, well, he left California this afternoon on a private plane. So, now you have to find him."

He nods, sober. "I will."

I'm sure he's right. I have complete faith in him. And I still feel like he owes me an apology for no-showing to our meeting earlier.

As if he reads minds, too, he meets my gaze. "I'm sorry about this morning. It won't happen again."

"Dune, I don't care what you do on your off-time, but when I call you in, you show up." I can pull a bitch when the occasion calls for it.

He rubs a hand across his stubbled jaw, still subtly glancing in all directions without moving his head. "Yeah. I was... incapacitated."

I arch a brow. "Was she that good?"

His head draws back, and his brows slam down. "What?" His laugh is unexpected—maybe to both of us. I detect relief in it which I file away to examine later. "No, it wasn't a woman—I wish." He gives his head a quick shake. "I mean —" He stops, his jade eyes meeting mine.

For a second neither of us speaks, gazes tangled, locked. Something flutters in my belly. His nostrils flare, and I watch the same trick of the light make his eyes flash blue. My lips part in surprise, and his gaze dips there.

"It wasn't a woman." His voice is deeper than I remember.

"What was it, then?" My voice has lost all authority—it sounds pathetically breathy to my ears.

He shakes his head. "Something else." He suddenly looks tired, almost defeated.

I'm shocked by a need to soothe him, a need to know what demons haunt this brave warrior. What does he hide under that impenetrable mask of deadly capability?

"Listen." He touches my nape, just under where the halter top ties. Energy shoots through me at the light contact, tingles of pleasure racing across my skin. I know this is just for show—we're playing the part of a flirty beach couple, but the thrumming that starts between my legs doesn't understand that. "I want to thank you for the help you gave me last month. You helped save a kidnapped child, so... it made a difference."

My mind wants to run down the path of figuring out whose child he was saving—his, a friend's—but all I can focus on is the light circles he traces on my skin. My breath hitches.

"I'm glad it helped."

"I owe you one. Call it in when you need it."

My nipples tighten. "Oh, I will." The confidence returns to my voice, but for some inexplicable reason, I choose this moment to blush. Maybe because of his penetrating stare as if he's trying to decipher what possible reason I might have for requesting a favor from him.

I hope to God I'll never need to. But the file I extracted for him isn't the only redacted data I've hacked. And considering which department of the government I work for, consequences could be more than a slap on the wrist. You never know.

So, having a friend capable of protecting my life could come in handy.

"You've uploaded the information to me?" he asks, tapping my tablet, back to business.

"Yes." I nod. "Let me know when it's done."

"Of course." He starts to step away, then turns back. "Annabel."

He's never called me by my first name before. It has an effect on me like he has me by the throat—but in a good way. He commands my full attention—my stiff nipples throb, tingles race over my skin.

"Are you in some kind of trouble?"

I hesitate, then shake my head. *Not yet.*

He nods. "You'll tell me when I need to know."

Then he's gone, blending into the crowd of people, and disappearing as quickly as he appeared.

Right. I'll tell him when he needs to know.

I truly hope that time won't come.

Why, then, does the idea of *not* sharing my secret with him disappoint me?

nnabel

I SIT in the L.A. office which I mostly share with National Resource Division employees. My direct boss works out of Langley, so I'm the only security professional here, and like Charlie, I'm entirely self-supervised.

Which gives me the means and time for personal investigation projects. I've been working on one since last October when I tried hacking into my own personnel records and came across my father's instead. Which was strange since my father never worked for the CIA.

Or so I thought.

And his records were sealed. All I saw was he was killed in the line of duty in El Salvador. That part matches what my family was told at the time. My father was a Major in the Marines who had been shot in El Salvador while on security detail for a high-level government official.

Supposedly.

So, what was he really doing in El Salvador for the CIA? Spying? Was my father an active agent? It appears so. I try for the thirty-fifth time to get in some backdoor to find the information. I have a degree in IT, and my ten years working for the CIA has taught me quite a bit about the department's info security system.

But I've been trying to hack this for months without much luck. It might be time to attempt a more direct route for information. I pick up the phone to dial CIA Director Edward Scape, my boss's boss. He's worked for the CIA for over forty years which means he would've been around when my father was here. He might be able to give me some kind of information.

I get the guy's secretary. "I'm sorry, Director Scape isn't available, may I take a message?"

I tap my fingernail on my keyboard, certain he's not going to call me back unless I give him a compelling reason. "May I have his voicemail, please?"

She hesitates, then says, "Sure. I'll send you there now."

Of course, anything on voicemail is going to be recorded. I have to think about what I'm going to say. "Hello, Agent Scape, this is Agent Annabel Gray from the Los Angeles office. I'm not actually calling about my current job detail, I'm calling about something personal. I came across information confirming my father, Major Jack Gray was a CIA agent in clandestine services. I was wondering if I could have access to his file or if you could fill me in on what he did here? You can check my security clearance. I won't let the information out anywhere. It's only for... personal reasons. For closure. I was just a girl when he died, and I had no idea we shared a career interest. I'd love to know more about him." I leave my phone number and thank him and hang up.

Then I tap my keyboard some more. He's probably not going to call.

Charlie

I FIND FRANGELICO IN TUCSON, of all places.

It seems a strange coincidence since the pack of wolves I followed last month are headquartered in Tucson. I'm not really the kind of guy who believes in the universe guiding your moves or anything, but it does scream an opportunity.

I could go and talk to Jared about what I am.

But even as I think it, I reject the idea. I'm not the kind of guy who asks for help from others, and I definitely don't want to align myself with these people—creatures—whatever they are. They're into questionable legal activity—cage fighting and who knows what else.

Do I want to know what happens when the moon is full? Do they hunt and kill like I did? And is their prey something far more significant than a rabbit? These are questions I'm not sure I want the answers to, not when I can barely accept what I am—what I've become.

Then again, keeping myself in the dark seems like a particularly stupid move, too.

Frangelico booked a room in a resort on the west side of town—Marriott Starr Pass. I head up there and swipe a key card from a housekeeping cart to get into his room.

Bugging the place is easy work but probably not that useful. I drop devices into the hem of his clothing and under the inner sole of his shoe. Really, though, I need to get the guy's phone. That's the best place for a bug and the most difficult to get.

Hearing a keycard slide into the lock, I slip out onto the balcony and press my back against the wall. It's my dumb luck, he comes straight my way. Maybe he saw the curtain move, maybe he just wants fresh air. Either way, I need to disappear. I drop over the side of the balcony, hanging by my fingertips as he stands there, sniffing.

Yeah, I can hear him sniff. My hearing has amplified since I first shifted under Jared's command last month.

I draw in a breath through my nose, picking up his scent as well. My sense of smell has increased, too. Frangelico smells odd—not at all like a person. More like a cold, earthy smell. It's... wrong.

I walk my hands quietly around the corner of the balcony and drop softly onto the balcony directly below. I sense rather than see Frangelico leaning over the side like he heard my movement, but I dart back into the shadows.

The guy is definitely on high alert. I jimmy the lock on the balcony door and slip out through the room below. I need a better plan to get to this guy, and I'd better think it through. He may not be surrounded by security, but the guy is cautious, maybe even paranoid. Which means he's definitely into something illegal.

I move quickly through the halls of the hotel and down to the front desk. Using one of my many fake IDs, I book a room for the night—right down the hall from his.

Annabel

"Ms. Gray? This is Director Scape."

I sit up taller, surprised. "Yes, Director Scape. Thank you so much for calling me back."

"So, you want to know about Major Gray."

"I do. Did you know him?"

"I did." He lets the words settle, and a queasy feeling turns in my belly.

"I'm sure things are classified, but can you tell me what he did for the CIA? How he really died?"

The director is silent for a moment. "Ms. Gray. Sometimes it's better not to know things about the deceased. The story you heard is probably a better one than anything I could say. Why not remember your father as a military hero?"

I don't like the implication. Is he saying my father *wasn't* a military hero?

"What are you telling me, Director Scape?"

"I'm saying, your father was an agent. You're an agent, Ms. Gray, but you've never worked in the field."

"No," I say faintly. Where's he going with this?

"Field agents make tough decisions. Sometimes they go rogue, let their own agendas affect their actions."

I suddenly can't breathe.

My father was a *rogue* agent? He did something wrong? Something bad?

"I'm a handler for field agents," I say tightly. "I know the things we might ask of them."

"Yes, and sometimes, agents go off the rails, Ms. Gray. They take actions that weren't part of the directive. Mistakes happen. That's what I'm saying. Your father's files are redacted. I'm not going to give you access to them, and I'm telling you if I did, you wouldn't like what you found. Forget about your father's last mission. Remember him as a hero, the way you always have. That's my advice to you."

My stomach is tighter than a drum. "I see," I say faintly.

"Ms. Gray?"

"Yes, sir?"

"How did you discover your father was an agent?"

My pulse picks up speed. I can't tell him I hacked the CIA's database. I'll lose my job. "I, um, found a journal of his. It's cryptic—he wouldn't have recorded government secrets—but I, I recognized some code words." Oh my God, I'm the worst liar ever.

Scape is quiet for a moment. "That journal is government property. I need you to return it to me as soon as possible."

My mind casts about wildly. "I already destroyed it." I'm proud of how even and confident my voice sounds. "I know these sorts of things shouldn't exist."

"I see." I'm not sure he believes me. "Well, I want you to forget about this. Stop looking, stop asking questions. Understood?"

The knot in my stomach unwinds a fraction of an inch. There's something off about his directive. "Yes, sir." I lightly tap my keyboard again.

"That's all." He hangs up without a goodbye.

I stare at my screen for a long time without seeing it. I'm tempted to call my sister, to ask her if she remembers anything, but she's not going to. My father wouldn't have been careless. If I know nothing, then surely my sister knows just as little. And we'll never know what our mother knew because she died last year of ovarian cancer.

My father's death involved something ugly. That's the only conclusion I can draw from my conversation with Director Scape. He wouldn't have warned me off the whole thing if there wasn't some big secret the government doesn't want anyone to know.

I consider his words. *Do* I want to know if my father did something awful? Something immoral? Something possibly related to innocent lives being lost?

I tap my keyboard—a nervous habit I should really stop.

Well, I'm not the kind of person to hide her head in the sand. If my father did something morally repugnant, I still want to know. Believing in a lie won't make my life any better.

Of course, finding out the truth could make it worse.

But something about the way Director Scape spoke to me has me on the defensive. Now, I want to know just because he warned me off. I'm stubborn like that. And he is an idiot if he thinks a CIA agent trained to dig up information is going to stop searching just because he tells her to. Especially, when he essentially confirmed there's something to find.

Charlie

I GET the tracking device into Frangelico's phone using the old jostle and pickpocket method when we pass by each other in the bar, returning it a few moments later when I emerged from the men's room.

By the time I get back to my room to get it online, I find the bug is dead.

Which probably means I've been made. Maybe I was made back on the balcony. The guy definitely seems to have a sixth sense.

A thought occurs to me that sends goosebumps prickling up my skin.

Could he be one of... *us*? Ugh. I can't believe I'm even saying *us*. But there's no denying it—I'm a monster like the rest of them, a man-beast who can't control his own urges.

Jared seemed to know I was a wolf by my scent. I haven't refined my new senses enough to distinguish anything, but suppose this guy Frangelico could? Suppose he scented or heard me out on his balcony?

I can smell the difference between male and female now. Hell, I'm fairly certain I can smell the scent of arousal on a female. That thought shouldn't bring the image of the lovely Annabel Gray to mind, but it does.

I've met with her before—dozens of times. But this last time, maybe because of my enhanced senses, everything seemed so vivid. The color of her long thick hair—dyed dark auburn and pulled back from her face with one single lock hanging down across her cheek, the smoothness of her skin, those big black eyeglass frames she wears that give her the sexy librarian look.

And her scent.

Really, I think that's what did me in.

She smelled like... heaven.

I had to snatch her ice cream out of her hand because if I didn't, I was going to try to devour *her*. The big bad wolf eating out his sexy handler.

I wanted to untie that halter top and let the scrap of fabric covering her breasts fall to the sand and see how pink her nipples are against that moon-pale skin. And that thought has me picturing what I'd have to do next—run the tip of my tongue between her breasts to find out if she tastes as good as she smells.

The next jumble of images that crowd my brain raise a

snarl in my throat. Annabel on her hands and knees with me behind her, riding hard. Her hair wrapped around my fist like a leash.

Jesus, fuck. I'm not that guy. I'm respectful to women. I don't throw them down and take what I want like some kind of... beast. Fuck. But I am a beast now, aren't I? And the urges are only getting stronger.

Is that what my father did to impregnate my mother? Did he force himself on her? Was that why she was always scared of him? Christ, I wish I could talk to her. Ask her about what happened, but she thinks I died in combat ten years ago. The government faked my death and gave me a new identity. I can't show up like a ghost and demand answers.

I consider texting her now just to report my current situation, but that's stupid. I won't report until the job is done, and it sure as hell isn't complete yet.

In fact, I'm fairly certain I've fucked it up. Which means my life is in danger.

But that's nothing new.

What's new is thinking people are something more than people, something different from human. The mind-fuck of finding out I'm a werewolf has me doubting every reality I've ever known, thinking my mark might be some kind of paranormal.

That's stupid.

He's a criminal who knows I'm after him. Just like any other marks. I just need to figure out another way to bug him.

I follow him out of the resort to the parking garage. And I totally lose him. I mean, he vanishes, completely. No cars start up, I hear no sound of footsteps.

But he's gone.

Dammit.

Annabel

MY BOSS, Lucy Tentrite calls me at work the next morning. Her voice is tight. "Annabel, I heard you called Director Scape."

"Yes, ma'am, that's true. It was for a personal matter."

"Yes, your father's death. Listen, I'm going to level with you as your boss and as a friend. I don't know what you're poking into, but between you and me, they don't like it. I'm giving you a direct order—drop the investigation. Are we clear?"

"Wow. Okay."

"You know the business we're in. We trade in secrets. There's some secret there, and it's above your pay grade. It doesn't matter if it involved your father. They don't want you to see it."

I don't say anything because really... what do you say to that?

"You've been searching internal records—ones you shouldn't have had access to. I could have your job for that. Hell, I could have you *prosecuted* for it."

I catch my breath. *They found out.*

"Leave it alone."

"Yes, ma'am."

"What's the word on Lucius Frangelico?" She changes the subject abruptly.

"Our operative is still in play."

"What's taking so long?"

I've wondered the same thing. I've had no check-in from Dune although that's not unusual. He won't call until the job is done. "I don't know. I'll find out."

"Do that. And update me."

"Yes, ma'am."

Because I'm shaken, not because I like to reach out to the hunky agent, I text a message to Dune. "Headquarters wants an update."

To my surprise, he calls immediately. "Secure line?"

"Switching." I reroute his call to a burner phone I keep for talking with agents. "Go ahead."

"What are you holding back about this guy?"

I pause to cover my surprise. Quickly, I open the Lucius Frangelico file and scroll through it for clues. I tap my finger lightly on the keyboard as I read.

"Annabel?"

He used my first name again. I shouldn't love it so much.

"I'm here, just trying to figure out what you mean."

"Every bug I've dropped he's destroyed within minutes. This isn't an ordinary target."

"Okay. I see he has a propensity to disappear without a trace. Questionable comings and goings. Possible murders in which the victims may have been shot at close range *after* death.

"So, how were they actually killed?"

"Unknown. Their brains are usually blown out. In one case, a man was decapitated." I fight a wave of nausea as I flip through the photos. And guilt. Because I should have researched this case deeper myself before I sent Dune. I guess I was too wrapped up in my personal research.

"Does the organization actually know what they're after here, or is it a mystery investigation?"

"Unclear."

"Permission to terminate suspect if engaged?"

A prick of fear creeps up the back of my neck. I try not to worry about agents getting killed—especially because I'm the one sending them out, but a foreboding chills me. Dune knows he's in danger. Still, I give the only answer I can. "They want him alive."

Dune curses softly. "I need different technology. He sweeps for bugs. Everything I've dropped on him has been destroyed."

"I'll contact R & D."

"In the meantime, I'll stay on him personally."

That chill of foreboding returns. "Have you been made, Charlie?" Now I'm using first names, too.

He blows out a breath. "Possibly."

Again, ice cold fear, like fingers squeezing my heart. I speak without thinking. "Come back in. I'll reassign it."

"The mission's not lost yet."

"Get back to L.A. That's an order."

Dune makes a noise that sounds like *huh* and says, "Copy that."

I end the call, trying to shake the bad feeling I have. I'm not one to believe in intuition, but it seems like something's telling me Charlie's in danger.

Which makes me think of my dad's death again. I've been mulling it over, and I remembered an old family friend, Sean Flack. He was a Marine, like my dad, but when I applied to the CIA, my mom said I should call him because he'd gone on to become the director of the agency. I hadn't called because I don't believe in using personal favors to get a job.

Sean was at my dad's funeral. I remember him standing in his crisp suit, comforting my mom. After I joined the CIA, he left and become a politician. He's a senator now.

I search for him in the CIA database.

Status: Retired. File redacted. Just like my father's. No surprise there.

Would he talk to me? I don't even know how I'd get through to him, but maybe he was good enough friends with my dad, he'll give me a few minutes of his time.

I call his office. "Yes, this is Annabel Gray, daughter of Major Jack Gray. My father and Senator Flack were Marine buddies. I really need to speak to Senator Flack about my father's death. Would you have him call me?"

"I will relay the message and see if the senator is available."

"Thank you." I leave my number and hang up.

If this lead gets me nowhere, I don't know what other tree to bark up. I guess I keep trying to hack the system. Or make a personal visit to Langley to break into the paper files.

Yeah, right. Like I know anything about stealing things in person. I'm a desk jockey, nothing more. Something like that would require field agent skills.

Charlie Dune's skills.

Maybe I'm ready to call in that favor after all.

A message blinks on my screen. Agent down in Tucson. Lucius Frangelico suspected of the murder.

Holy shit. It could've been Charlie.

Thank God, I called him back.

3

I DRIVE BACK to California and go to my small apartment.

The mountains are calling me. I had the urge to shift and run in Tucson but held it together. I was on a job. Now, with nothing to fill my time, I can't stop thinking about it.

It's either that or beat down agent Annabel Gray's door because I can't seem to get her scent out of my nostrils or the dirty thoughts out of my mind.

Fuck. I have to get myself under control.

My phone blinks with an incoming call. Annabel's burner phone. "Dune speaking."

"Charlie?" Annabel sounds breathless, frightened.

Immediately, my senses go haywire—adrenaline spiking, heat flushing through. My cells try to rearrange like my body wants to shift to wolf form. I suck in a deep breath and force the urge back down.

"Annabel? Where are you?" She has trackers on me which I already shut off because the mission was aborted, but I don't have any on her.

"In my apartment. Can you meet?"

I'm already out the door, running for my vehicle. My brain flashes over a million scenarios. "Do you have a gun? Can you get somewhere safe?"

I hear the tremble in her inhale, but her voice is calm. "Yes and yes. I think so."

I jump in the truck and start it up, cursing myself for not already changing this vehicle out for another one. "Are you alone?"

"Yes, but someone's been here." Her voice raises on the last word.

"All right. Sit down where you can see all the entrances and exits and keep your gun cocked and in your hand. Understand? Stay calm. What's your address?"

I'm relieved when I hear it's not far from mine. "I'll be there in twenty minutes. Call back if you hear or see anything."

"Okay. Okay. I will." I can't stand the fear in her voice.

The fact she called me rather than the cops tells me she's into something, which I'd already suspected. And if a CIA agent is into something, it has to be deep. Because we're already on our own questionable side of the law.

Danger usually makes me calm. I'm the sort of guy they sent into diffuse bombs in the war because I practically go serene under pressure, but thinking of Annabel in danger has me keyed up. Or maybe it's the fucking wolf in me— maybe both. Either way, I have to work hard to find my usual Zen.

I get there in fifteen minutes by stealth racing through the back routes of the city. I don't see any cars that look like surveillance, but they could be anywhere—someone in an apartment across the street or one of the people walking by. I park around the corner and grab a plumber's shirt and toolbox out of the trunk for a quick cover. Adopting a slight limp, I head into the building.

It's an open-air apartment building where all the doors open to outside landings. I take the concrete steps up the side, lumbering as if my hip causes me pain. When I find her apartment, I knock. "CD Plumbing," I say, hoping she'll figure out the *CD* stands for *Charlie Dune*. We have a code phrase, but for some reason, I don't want to drop it.

My newly enhanced hearing detects movement inside. She must be right up at the door. I lift the bill of my hat so she can see my eyes through the peephole, and she pulls open the door with an audible exhale. She has the government-issue pistol in her hand, and she's wearing a business suit like she just came home from the office.

"You have a leak, ma'am?" I step inside and wait for her to shut the door. The place has been trashed—books pulled down from bookshelves, cabinets emptied. Someone was searching for something. The moment I'm in, I drop the plumbing supplies and draw my gun, checking to make sure the place is clear even though it must be. Only when I'm sure—by both my traditional methods and my newly developing sense of smell—do I speak.

"What's going on?"

Despite her fear, she's all business. I'd expect nothing less of Agent Gray. She's a smart and capable young woman.

"Entered through the front door. I found it unlocked. Charlie—look at this." She leads me to the bedroom and points at a framed photograph lying on her pillow. At first, I think it's her with what must be her son, but then I realize the woman in the photo only resembles her—a sister then.

"Any prints?"

"I haven't touched it. I didn't touch anything. I just called you."

That shouldn't make me feel a foot taller, but it does.

I go back to my plumber's toolbox and lift the basic tool tray away to reveal my more specialized tools. I dust the photograph for prints, but there are none. Same goes with the front door knob.

"What are they looking for?"

Fear flashes in her eyes, but she shakes her head. "I don't know."

A lie.

"Anything missing?"

"No."

"Who's in the photo?"

Tears immediately pop into Annabel's eyes, and she turns away to hide them. "My sister, Sarah and my nephew, Grady. And Dune—" she drags in a shaky breath. "I can't get them on the phone."

I take her shoulders and turn her back to face me. "The photo is a warning. What is this about?"

She blinks rapidly, her throat working. "I've been investigating something. Something personal. They told me to stop."

"And you didn't."

She nods.

"The *organization* told you to stop." I want to be clear we're dealing with CIA here.

"Right."

"Okay, this is a classic scare tactic." I pace around the room looking for more clues.

"It's a warning, not direct action. If they'd actually harmed your sister and nephew, you'd know it. So, they're somewhere. We need to find them and put them out of reach."

"All right. Good." Annabel's shoulders inch down, her lips stop trembling. "I'm glad I called you—really glad."

I consider her. "I'd do this for you even if I didn't owe you the favor. You should know that. But Annabel?"

"Yes?" She lifts gray eyes to meet mine.

"I need the whole story. What you're researching—who's involved."

She takes a small step backward and angles her body away from mine. "It's an internal thing. You don't need to know in order to protect my family."

The growl that comes out of my throat surprises me. It's an animal sound. I grab her arm and spin her around to face me.

"This isn't a job. It's personal—for you and for me. You don't get to call that *need to know* bullshit with me."

Her lips press together. I don't think she's a natural redhead, but she sure as hell has the stubbornness to match her beautiful auburn locks.

"It will put you in more danger."

I let out a harsh laugh and walk toward her, backing her up until she hits the wall. I lean on one hand beside her head, caging her in.

"There's one thing I won't accept from you, Annabel —lies."

I swear to Christ, her eyes dilate like she's turned on, rather than scared. I don't know if turning her on was my intent before, but it sure as hell is now. I press forward, even more, letting the heat of my body brush against hers.

"You're the one in danger here, not me. You and your family. Don't pretend I require protection, sweetheart. You want my help, all the cards go on the table. Otherwise, I'm walking out that door right now."

It's not true. There's no way in hell I'd leave Annabel in trouble and unprotected, but hopefully, she doesn't know enough about me to be sure.

I'm a highly trained special agent. I speak twelve languages fluently, know fifty-three ways to kill a man with my bare hands, but nothing in my training prepared me for Annabel yanking my mouth down to hers like her life depended on it.

No one calls me slow though. I have her shirt off and her bra down in five seconds flat as she sucks my lower lip into her mouth. One of her long legs is around my waist, and she's grinding her hot pussy over my cock.

Of course, I'm considering every angle. I'm not stupid. This could be a calculated move to distract me from my line of questioning. Or a more sinister ploy—maybe the whole thing is a trap to get me into her place and nail me with something. But I taste desperation in her kisses, wild, frenzied need.

If I can trust my gut, I'd say Annabel is upset and needs this release. And if I'm wrong? Well, I can handle myself against whatever she pulls. I've escaped from literally hundreds of deaths. I cup her breasts and thrust my hardened cock against the notch between her legs. Her scent gets up in my nostrils, and I sense the monster inside me throwing himself against the cage bars.

Her soft lips move like her life depends on the kiss—quick, hungry twists and pulls. Her short skirt rides up to her waist, leaving just a thin pair of panties between me and her delectable pussy.

"You need me to fuck you?" I rasp against her throat as she kisses along my neck, bites my shoulder.

She gives her head a shake like she's snapping out of something. "Uh, I don't know." Suddenly, she's unsure again, fumbling and scared.

No.

I'm not going to let that happen. She wanted something from me, and I'm going to deliver it. I cup her ass and keep her in the perfect position.

"Say *no* if you want me to stop," I rumble against her ear. "Otherwise, I'm going to help you forget. Give you a release."

"Yes," she breathes. "Make me forget. Just for a moment."

That's all I need. I bounce her higher on the wall, so my lips reach her perky nipple. It *is* peachy-pink—just like I imagined, so perfect and delicate. I suck on it until it gets hard, then release it and flick it with my tongue.

Her fingers burrow through my hair, and she arches and moans. Her breath comes fast with little needy cries on the exhales.

Fuck it. Maybe this is the right time to be an animal. I shake a condom out of my wallet while Annabel attacks me with her lips, her teeth.

"Christ, Annabel," I curse. "Christ." I get my dick out, and the condom rolled on while keeping her nailed to the wall which I'm pretty sure takes more skill than the average guy has.

"*Now,* Charlie."

Oh God. I fucking love her getting bossy with me. Her desperation tears at me, fills me with the need to please her like no man ever has. But I don't have time for that. This will have to be satisfying in that crazy impassioned way.

I shove her panties to the side. One thrust and I'm deep inside her. She chokes on her gasp, and I stop, somehow dialing it back. "You okay?" I manage to say.

"*Move,* Charlie. Please."

Yes, ma'am. That's all the encouragement I need. I fuck her hard against the wall, ramming up into her with every thrust, holding her captive so I can drill deeper every time.

"Is this what you need, sweetheart?"

She digs her nails into the back of my neck and shakes her head. "Harder. Harder. Make it hurt."

Make it hurt?

My need to satisfy her collides with the southern gentleman in me, the respectful soldier. Satisfaction wins out—or maybe it's my goddamn wolf. Either way, I'm no longer capable of holding back. I fuck her so hard, I'm surprised I don't bust a hole in the wall with her ass, and she takes it. She takes every savage stroke until she's climbing me, screaming, begging in incoherent babble.

I squeeze her breast, pinch her nipple. When I twist and pull, she comes, a keening cry issuing from her throat.

I come, too, thrusting deep and staying there for my release.

We breathe together, face to face, mouths touching but not kissing. I pick up the beat of her heart, thudding against her chest. Her scent consumes me. Even though I've already had her, I have the insane urge to rub my entire body over hers, covering her in my scent—marking her, so other males know to stay away.

But that's nuts.

Annabel

THE ROOM SPINS. I'm lightheaded from the orgasm or maybe

from the heat—I can't tell. Fortunately, Charlie doesn't let me go. He keeps me pinned against the wall, his cock still filling me as we both pant to recover our breaths.

His eyes look blue again although there's no sunlight hitting them now.

I don't feel guilty I just had sex while my sister and nephew are missing. Hell, if anything, I can rationalize I did this *for* them. I couldn't think before, I was so wracked with fear. I needed this.

And if I were the conniving type, which I'm not, I would say it was a good move to bond Charlie and further gain his sympathy. But that's not why I did it.

I don't know why he did it, but I don't care. I'm not going to ask anything more of him. Not going to expect a relationship—which he could never deliver. I just needed this human contact. Just needed to feel his support in this visceral, cathartic way.

After a few moments, he eases out of me and lowers me to my feet. When he straightens my skirt, my chest squeezes a little at being cared for. It's been a very long time since anyone did anything for me.

"You ready to talk, baby?" He leans his forehead against mine as he deftly removes the condom and buttons up his pants with one hand.

It's not really a question, it's a demand. I talk, or he walks. I love how commanding he is—how he manages to still be respectful at the same time.

"Okay," I croak.

He leaves to dispose of the condom, and I feel the loss of him acutely. I still have the wall to hold me up, yet nothing will keep me from sliding down it and crumpling in a scared little ball on the floor.

But then he's back, offering his hand. He leads me to a

take a seat on my sofa, and he pulls up the ottoman to sit right in front of me—interrogator to detainee.

No, that's not what this is. My reluctance to tell him my father may have done something bad is not a good enough reason to keep silent. He's going to help me. I can tell him what I know. I run my fingers through my hair which must be a mess after our escapade against the wall.

"I found out my dad was CIA. I thought he died in the service, but I guess that was a cover. He was on some kind of operation in El Salvador."

Charlie watches me, that ever-alert awareness to his entire body. He's so still—there's no fidgeting, no movement, almost like a predator right before it pounces.

"I was digging around, trying to get into redacted files—same thing I did for you with the lab fire cases, only I couldn't get much. So, I got bold and made a few phone calls."

Charlie purses his lips. "And?"

"I called Director Scape. He told me to back off. That I might not like what I found out. Let sleeping dogs lie, that kind of thing."

Charlie still doesn't move.

"The next day I get a call from Agent Tentrite. She tells me she'll prosecute if I hack any more internal files."

He absorbs the information and waits. Not one to spend a useless word, this guy.

"This morning I called Senator Flack. He was at my father's funeral. They were friends. He didn't call back. When I got home, I found this." I indicate the wrecked apartment and the bedroom with the photo. Tears pop into my eyes again as fear for my sister and nephew spikes.

"But what were they looking for here? Did you print anything out? Transfer files?"

I shiver. Acknowledging this fact makes everything so much more real. "I said I found a journal of my father's. It wasn't true, but I didn't want to admit I'd hacked files."

Charlie purses his lips and nods. "So, they want the journal. They may not stop until they get it."

"I don't have it!" My voice rises in pitch before I force myself to take a breath.

My phone rings and I snatch it up. "Sarah!" I cry when I see my sister's name on the screen. I swipe right and answer. "Oh my God, where have you been?"

"Hey girl!" I hear nothing but cheeriness in her voice. "We're here! Can't wait to hit Disneyland."

"Wh-what?"

"What an incredible surprise. Grady is over the moon. Thanks so much for swinging this, but next time a little heads' up would've helped. I had a big project at work, and I had to call in sick to get here."

"Wait, where are you?" I stand up, already grabbing my purse. Dune is right behind me as if he heard every word.

"We're in Anaheim already. We took the hotel shuttle, checked in and came straight to the park. Didn't you say to meet you at Space Mountain? Why all the cloak and dagger, anyway?"

"Uh, so you're at Space Mountain now?"

"Yeah, but I don't see you."

"Right. I'm not there yet, but I'm on my way."

"Tell her to get lost in the crowd," Dune whispers.

"Don't wait for me. Go ride a bunch of rides, and I'll call you when I get there. Okay? Get busy, and I'll find you."

"When are you going to tell me what this is all about? Why the big surprise?"

"Go!" I practically shout, then dial it back in. My sister's phone is probably bugged. My phone is probably bugged. "I'll see you soon."

"Okay, whatever! See you soon." Sarah hangs up, and I grab Dune's arm.

"They have my sister," I whisper in a choked voice.

"No. This is a mindfuck." He shakes his head and touches my shoulder. "If they wanted to hurt her, they would have. This is an elaborate game to scare you. Either that or they plan to hold her hostage for the non-existent journal."

I stare at him, my heart racing. "This just keeps getting worse and worse," I whisper. "And the minute I called you in, I declared war."

"Yeah," he nods, grimly. "So, we're going to get to Sarah and Grady before they do." He takes the phone out of my hand, drops it to the ground and steps on it, crushing the electronics. "Only the burner phone from now on."

I nod.

"You go first. Take my keys. My truck is parked on the street south of the building. Get in and drive to the west side. Pick me up there. I'll see you in two-point-five minutes."

I have to force myself to gape at the precision of his instructions. There's no time to marvel. I have two-point-five minutes to follow his orders. I move briskly out of my apartment and down the stairs. I'm paranoid, so every single human being I see looks like an agent watching me—even the little old lady walking her miniature schnauzer.

No one stops me. I get in the truck, start it up, and drive to the west side. Charlie emerges out of nowhere and gets in. He directs me through the Los Angeles streets toward Anaheim.

I'm a nervous mess, but his calm, clipped instructions

keep me sane, focused. He drops the passenger side shade and uses the mirror in it to watch behind us.

"Turn into this alley," he commands sharply.

I squeak and make the turn, my tires screeching on the pavement. "Are we being followed?"

"That's an affirmative."

He takes his gun out and cocks it.

"What are you doing?" I wail. Things have escalated too fast. I know shootouts happen. I know car chases happen, but they don't usually involve me. He rolls down the window and aims at the car that turned into the alleyway after us.

"Just slowing him down." He fires and the car behind us swerves.

"Turn right, back to the main street. Step on it," he commands.

They return fire as I make the turn, but nothing hits us.

"Did you shoot someone?" I know I don't sound like a CIA agent, but I'm rapidly going into shock here.

"No, I shot their tire. I'm not going to shoot one of our own unless I'm sure they're going to kill one of us. And I don't believe they have orders for that."

"Th-this could be someone we know." The thought occurs to me with a sinking sensation. It's not some nameless enemy.

"Yeah. I couldn't see their faces, but that's another reason I think we're safe enough. If a kill order had been issued, we'd know it."

He speaks with such certainly. I have to trust he knows what's going on here. He's usually the guy doing the chasing.

It takes me an hour to get to Anaheim. We park and get out. "You know what the worst thing about this is?"

"What?" Charlie asks, eyes scanning the parking lot, the park, every bit of our surroundings.

"I've been talking to Sarah about bringing Grady to Disneyland since I moved here three years ago. I never made it happen and now—"

"Now they're fine. You'll have a chance to take them later."

I lean into his quiet authority. Hope to God he's right.

"Right now, you're going to call your sister. Figure out a place to meet without saying it if you can."

My fingers tremble as I call my sister's number.

"Hello?" She doesn't recognize the burner phone number.

"Hey, I'm here. Meet me at the ride I puked on when we were little." I end the call before she can answer.

Charlie's lips twitch. "Good work." He pulls my suit jacket off and rips open my blouse, popping all the buttons off.

"Hey!" I yelp, even though I know what he's doing.

"Sorry. I'll buy you a new one," he says. He ties the two ends of the blouse at my waist, leaving my camisole exposed in front. Then he rolls the waistband of my skirt down a couple times, shortening the length of my skirt by several inches. He hands me his ball cap. "Any chance you can get all that hair underneath this?"

I guess dying my long hair dark red wasn't my smartest move. Way too recognizable. I twist it up into a knot on the top of my head and pull the cap over. It doesn't quite fit—my hair overstuffs the hat—but at least it's covered.

"You need those glasses to see?" he asks, starting to take them off.

"Yes," I jerk out of his reach.

His lips twitch again. "All right. Keep the cap low." He

throws his plumber shirt into the truck, transforming into hot Disney dad in an aqua t-shirt and jeans. He buys us entrance tickets, and we head in.

"I'm gonna guess Space Mountain." He raises his eyebrows in inquiry and slightly amused look. It's nice to see him without the blank super agent expression. Nice to know there's a real guy underneath the warrior armor.

I let out a nervous laugh. "Actually, no. It's A Small World."

"Come on, you have to be kidding." Even though we're bantering, we walk fast, almost jogging. My hand is in his like we're a couple on a date, and he smiles encouragingly like we're running because he can't wait to show me something, not because innocent lives are at stake here.

Clever, clever man.

"No. I ate too much ice cream and got overheated. I threw up right in the boat."

Charlie winces as he navigates smoothly through the throngs of people. We're surrounded by the din of music and people, the smells of sweet confections and body odor. He gets us to the ride in record time.

"There!" I point. My sister and Grady stand in front of the ride, Sarah's arms folded over her chest, annoyance tightening her face.

Charlie's scanning, scanning everywhere. "You get Grady. I'll take your sister. Meet at the truck in ten."

My feet scramble to catch up with the orders. Okay, so we're splitting up. Good plan. Charlie's already cruising right for Sarah.

"Sarah!" Grady exclaims as if they're long-lost friends. He opens his arms wide for a hug. Sarah flashes me a frown over his shoulder, right before he envelopes her.

"Hey, Grady!" My nephew runs to give me a hug. "Come

on, I want to show you the best ride, ever."

"I wanted to do Splash Mountain," he protests. "And we already had to get out of line to meet you here."

Charlie's already said something to Sarah and whisked her away. She knows where I work. If he told her she's in danger and he showed up with me, she should go along with it. Hopefully, I can wrangle Grady into listening, too.

"Grady, Grady, listen." I bend my knees to look him in the eyes. He's eight years old and a smart kid, he'll understand. "We're in trouble. Someone's after you and your mom and me. So, I just need you to pretend we're heading for a ride, but I'm going to get us out of here as fast as I can. Got it?"

His face goes pale, but he nods, immediately trotting beside me without another protest.

Good kid.

I see a guy move from a nearby railing and fall into step behind us.

Shit.

I yank Grady into a candy shop, then squirrel through to exit out the other side.

My tail is still there.

"Okay, Grady, they're following us. Any ideas?" Kids are way smarter than people give them credit for. And sometimes, they have ideas an adult would never consider.

He takes off sprinting at top speed. Well, that's one idea. I run to follow him.

The guy behind us also jogs to keep up.

Grady weaves in and out of people. I almost lose him myself and have to push to keep up with his agile darting.

We end up driving into a thicker mass of people and... the six p.m. parade.

Genius.

I don't know if Grady led us here on purpose, or it was just luck, but it's a perfect place to disappear. I trail my nephew as he ducks through the throng, then, miraculously, we're at the entrance.

"Great work, buddy. This way." I lead him toward the truck, hoping Sarah and Charlie had equal luck.

When I get near the truck, I find Charlie leaning against some other car, kissing Sarah.

~

Charlie

THERE'S a guy fifty yards away, scanning the parking lot. I kiss Sarah for cover, right when Annabel arrives.

For the record, they may be sisters, but Sarah neither tastes nor smells like Annabel. My body doesn't have the animalistic reaction I have to Annabel. Which means the lust I feel for her isn't just the emergent wolf in me. There's something more to this attraction.

While I work the kiss, I hold an electric lock opening device up to the door lock of the Lexus SUV we're leaned up against. We can't drive the truck out of here if we hope to escape unfollowed.

I break the kiss when the door beeps and pull the door open. "Get in," I order in the same low, calm voice I use for every command under pressure.

I take the driver's seat because, this time, we really need to lose any tail we pick up. Plus, I don't think I'll need to fire a gun. Hell, I'd better not have to fire a gun around Disneyland. I'm an excellent shot but taking chances with innocent children would kill me.

Annabel and Grady jump in seconds later. She takes the front passenger seat and glowers at me. I use the same device to start up the car and drive out of Disneyland, watching my speed, so I don't attract attention.

"I like your car," Grady says.

"It's not his," Annabel mutters. She snaps her gaze to me. "Did you just kiss my sister?"

"Yeah, do you even know each other?" Grady asks from the back seat.

"It was a pretend kiss, honey," Sarah chuckles drily, "because someone was looking at us."

Annabel's still glaring daggers at me which, I have to admit, turns me on. I like the idea of receiving her anger, soothing her. I like the idea of her jealous.

Way too much.

I don't know what the hell I'm doing with this woman, but I'm in way over my head.

I probably just gave up my job for her, for one thing. And I don't have the kind of job you can quit. You either retire, or you go out in a body bag. They don't like loose ends in the CIA. I don't think they're going to fire me and let me be out in the world with everything I know.

In fact, I'm sure they won't.

Of course, I have every means at my disposal to disappear permanently, so it's not that big a worry.

The bigger concern is the magnitude of my attraction to her, and what I'm going to do about it. Even if I don't lose my job over this, I don't live the kind of lifestyle that allows for a relationship. Even more, I don't even know if I'm safe for her to date.

Do werewolves attack people at full moons? That's the lore. I'm certainly finding my aggression and sexual desires mounting each day we draw closer to the full moon.

I glance over at Annabel, whose jaw is set, eyes pinned to the road. "I'm sorry." I use a low voice. "I won't do it again."

Surprise dances over her face followed closely by a pretty blush.

"I don't have a sister fetish, I promise." I reach over and squeeze her hand.

I think she wants to stay mad, but her lips tug up in a reluctant smile. And it's incredible what that smile does to me. I'm suddenly high over our escape, adrenaline bringing me a joy I don't usually allow myself to experience.

And touching her brings on an erection so hard, I have to shift in my seat to alleviate the discomfort.

Annabel—ever observant—glances down at it and back up at my face. Her smile grows.

"So, when are you going to tell me what in the hell is going on?" Sarah demands.

Right. Focus, Dune. Lives are at stake here.

Annabel turns in her seat to address Sarah. "Charlie and I work together. We had a mission in LA that might have been compromised."

A low rumble reaches my ears, and I realize I'm growling. I cut off the sound just as Annabel turns to me curiously.

Sarah pulls Grady in tight against her, but the youngster pushes his mom back off.

"Are you spies?" he asks.

"Yes, sort of," Annabel answers.

"So, the plane tickets—the trip to Disneyland—it was to get us safe? Why didn't you just tell me?"

"I didn't send the tickets."

Sarah pales and yanks Grady against her, this time ignoring his struggle. "So, now what?" she asks in a shaky voice.

"I'm taking you somewhere safe," I speak up. "And you'll have to stay there until Annabel and I get things figured out, so it's safe for you to go home."

Annabel shoots me a grateful look that makes my dick throb.

I drive them to my cabin in the mountains. It's the most secluded safehouse I have at the moment and a place I'd feel comfortable leaving Sarah and Grady alone. The only drawback—I don't know if I can contain the monster inside me once I'm up there. And I sure as hell don't know what will happen if I come dragging myself back naked and covered with blood when I'm done hunting.

I don't even consider my biggest fear because I'm the kind of guy who refuses to surrender to worry. But fuck, if there's any sign I'm a danger to these people, I'm going to have to leave them. Maybe even figure out a way to end my life which goes against every instinct in my body—I'm wired for survival at all costs.

Annabel

CHARLIE GETS quiet as he drives us up a dirt road winding up the mountain. Or maybe he's always this quiet. It seems strange that I don't know. I feel so close to him, and yet we haven't spent that much time together—very brief snippets over the past few years as his handler, and now, today, that's it.

The moon is half full, peeking through the trees as we wind higher. We arrive at a tiny, solitary cabin, tucked away from everything. It appears old and rustic, but there's a satellite on the roof and inside is simple but comfortable. Grady and I walk around, taking in the place. The cupboards are already stocked with enough non-perishables to last a month. Charlie stopped at a convenience store on the way up to pick up basics like milk, eggs, fruit, and bread.

A desk is against the wall of the living room, wired with the latest high tech, government-issue equipment.

There's only one bedroom.

"I'll take the couch," Charlie offers as if guessing where my thoughts are going. "You three can share the bed."

I'm not sure why I find that thought so disappointing. What did I think, I'd be having more sex with Charlie with my sister and nephew a few feet away?

Hard no. Sigh.

Besides, we're not on a date. We're on a mission.

I'm not certain why Dune picked such an out-of-the-way place for a safehouse. "Is this where you were when you said you spent the night out of the city?"

He looks over from the refrigerator where he's putting away groceries. "Yeah."

"Why?"

"I wanted to be alone. And I like to... explore out here."

Huh. Charlie Dune, mountain man. I had no idea, but it makes him all the more appealing.

There's a television, which I doubt Charlie watches, but he gets it hooked up and streams in the latest *Star Wars* movie for Grady. Then he beckons me to the desk. I follow because we need to talk.

"My sister and Grady—" I begin in a hushed voice, stepping close to him so we can whisper.

"Are on a *need-to-know* basis," he finishes for me. My skin prickles at his proximity. Even in normal clothes, Charlie could never be mistaken for a civilian. There's too much power, too much energy packed into his hard, muscled body. "I would never tell them anything that would put them in jeopardy."

I nod.

"Show me everything you have on this case."

This case.

It seems strange to call my father's death a "case," but I guess it is.

"All right. What I know is my father's death coincided with the signing of the Chapultepec Peace Accord ending the civil war in El Salvador. As I'm sure you know from your American history, our government had an interest in keeping the military-led government in place despite their horrific acts of violence and human rights abuses.

"The story I heard growing up was my father was on Marine security detail for one of the U.S. Government officials and was killed by a left-wing political activist. He was given a hero's burial. So, when I found out he was killed in the line of duty while on a mission for the CIA, I started digging.

"What mission did we have? Who really killed him? I don't know why I needed to know, but—"

Charlie waves his hand. "You don't need to explain yourself to me." His tone implies he understands too well the obsession that came over me to find the truth. "So, what did you find?"

"Absolutely nothing. So, I called Director Scape. And he —" I grind my teeth at the memory, my stomach twisting up in a knot.

Charlie's watching me closely. "Tell me everything," he warns like he knows this is the part I want to leave out.

"He implied my father went rogue and did something

bad. That I'd be better off remembering him as a hero because if I found out what really happened, it would change how I felt about him."

"Did you believe him?"

I shrug. "At first I did. But the way he ended the conversation, with such a strong warning not to keep looking, well —" I chew the inside of my cheek. "It made me suspicious. Of a cover-up."

"Okay. Then what?"

"He wanted to know how I found out my father was a covert operative. That's when I made up the journal thing. He said it was government property, and I had to turn it in, so I said I had already destroyed it."

"That was your mistake," Charlie says. "If you'd turned in something manufactured and innocuous, they might have put this to bed. Or even if you promised to turn something in."

I suck my cheek in between my teeth. "I could still do that. Call in and offer it. Apologize for everything. Maybe they'd let me keep my job."

"Yes. That's an option. It has risks."

"Which are?"

"There will certainly be disciplinary action, for both of us."

A spike of fiery regret slices through my belly. One phone call, one decision and I cost Charlie his job, possibly his freedom.

And he hasn't once complained or pointed it out to me.

"There may be manufactured charges or inflated ones. Enough to put us in jail and out of their way. Depends on how well you're trusted and who's willing to go to bat for you. Or how afraid they are of you discovering the truth."

"What about you?" I whisper.

He shrugs. "I'm useful to them. I might get a slap on the wrist, especially if I play you up as my lover."

I'm pretty sure the blood drains out of my face. Did he —? Is that why—?

"No," he says firmly as if he's guessed my thoughts. "I didn't have sex with you to cover my bases. Not even close." He speaks so certainly, with total conviction, I have no choice but to believe him. My anger drains away, leaving only raw vulnerability.

Damn my lips for trembling.

"Hey." His fingers tangle in the back of my hair, and he uses it to lift my face to his. His lips brush across mine. "Sex with you was completely out of my control. I didn't plan it, I don't know it if was wise, but there was no helping it. What I feel for you is pure, raw animal magnetism. The only thing that would've stopped me was you. I'll always respect your wishes. I hope you know that. It's not a requirement for my help."

Something rearranges in my chest. A warmth and light-ness steal through me like rays of sun after rain. "Thanks," I mumble and try to drop my head, but Charlie won't allow it. He keeps me captive in his iron grip, the gentleness in his expression in direct opposition to the dominating hold.

"Believe it, Annabel."

Tears pop into my eyes. "I do," I whisper.

He claims my mouth with the passion, the fervor of before. His lips drag across mine, open and close over mine, devouring me. "You're like an addiction," he murmurs when he's thoroughly taught me a lesson in submission, and my pussy is wet for him.

I wriggle in my chair, needing relief, but it's not destined to happen. I feel my sister's curious gaze on us from across the cabin and Grady's right there, too.

Damn.

"Keep talking," he orders, releasing my hair like nothing just happened. "There's more, isn't there?"

My voice shakes a little as I tell him about my boss calling and her direct warning, and about leaving a message with Senator Flack.

"What number did you leave for him to call you back on?"

I glance at my purse. "The burner phone."

Charlie's mouth quirks. "Good."

"So, what now? Should I call my boss? Tell her what's happened?"

Charlie has that blank expression on his face, which I believe means there's a shit-ton going on inside his head.

"You could. What do you predict will happen?"

"She'll tell me to come in. Set up a location to meet."

"And?" I get the feeling Charlie's asking only to force me to think this through, that he's already run every scenario available to me.

"Then, like you said, there could be disciplinary action. And there won't be answers. If I go in now, I'll never find out what happened."

He nods.

I clench my teeth. "I *need* to find out what happened. What they don't want me to know."

"Then we keep pressing," Charlie says. The fact he used *we* and not *you* nearly makes me weep with gratitude. "Sarah and Grady are safe. We investigate the clues we have. You can always call in later. Produce a fake journal and call a truce. It's an option. But not your only option."

I reach out to grab his hand. "Thank you."

4

C *harlie*

GRADY'S UP almost as early as I am, padding into the kitchen at the first light of dawn. I'll bet that drives his mom nuts.

"You hungry?" I ask.

He shrugs.

"I'm gonna take that as a yes." I set a box of Golden Grahams on the table with a bowl. "Have some cereal."

He seems to like that and tears open the box. The cereal spills on the table, but I don't say anything, just pour milk into his bowl and drop a spoon into it. "Have at it."

He shovels a bite into his mouth. "Thanks."

Sarah comes out next, but Annabel hits the shower. I get itchy thinking about her being naked with just a thin door between us. Last night, I had to leave the cabin because the desire to open that bedroom door and throw Annabel over my shoulder was too strong.

I shifted and hunted most of the night. I'm just glad I found my way back and was able to change back to human form before morning.

Annabel wanted to hack into the CIA last night, but she was drained from the stress of the day. She's hoping to crack it today.

Sarah stands at the window, looking out. "It's beautiful here."

"Where are you from?" I realize I don't know, just that they received plane tickets to fly to L.A. yesterday.

"Oklahoma."

The bathroom door opens, and Annabel emerges—in a goddamn towel. My entire body flushes with heat, and something wonky happens with my vision. Fuck—is it my wolf trying to come out?

What in the hell does that mean?

"Is it all right to leave the cabin? Could I take Grady out for a hike?"

I shove my hands in my pockets to hide my boner. "Yeah, sure. It's safe here."

"Okay, we'll be back in an hour or so." She turns to Grady, who's already out of his seat at the table, pulling on his shoes. "Ready, bud?"

"I'm ready. You're the one who's taking so long."

She rolls her eyes and pulls on a light jacket, and the two of them leave the cabin.

"Charlie?" Annabel calls from the bedroom.

"Yeah?"

"Can you come in here for a second?"

My hand goes to my pistol even though I don't smell or hear an intruder. Still, there's an oddness to Annabel's tone that has my skin prickling.

Then I nearly fall on my ass.

Because Annabel Gray is stark naked, pulling me into the bedroom. She drops to her knees and unbuckles my belt.

"Fuck," I mutter, drawing in breath to oxygenate my brain because all the blood just rushed south.

"I just wanted to thank you," she purrs as she frees my erection.

My hand tangles in her wet hair. "Oh yeah?" If I were a gentleman, I'd tell her no thanks was necessary, but there's no way in hell I can refuse this gift. Not after I spent the entire night fantasizing about exactly how her crimson lips would look stretched over my cock. She fists the base and sticks out her tongue, rubbing the head over it, just enough to moisten the taut skin.

I groan. "Don't tease," I pant. "Don't fucking tease. I've been hard for you since the second I took the condom off last time."

Her gray gaze lifts to meet mine, and she opens her mouth and engulfs my length.

I'm an asshole because the beast in me roars to the fore. I grab her by the hair to hold her still and thrust deep into her throat.

She gags, but still sucks hard when I pull out.

"Oh God," I groan. "That's so fucking good." I thrust again and again, relishing the heat, the way her tongue glides along the underside of my shaft, the way she hollows her cheeks to pull. "Annabel, it's not fair."

She pops off. "What's not fair?"

"You shouldn't be able to do this to me. It shouldn't be legal, it's too fucking good." I'm babbling like an idiot. It's so unlike me, but I can't seem to stop.

I tighten my grip in her hair and pump fast. My eyes roll back in my head.

Annabel's making little sounds around my cock. Aroused sounds. When she reaches her fingers between her legs, I growl.

She needs me there.

Now.

I pull out and lift her to her feet with unnatural strength. In a flash, she's on her back on the bed, and I yank her thighs until her ass reaches the edge.

She spreads them wide. *Beautiful.* So, beautiful. Naked and lush and perfect.

Condom. Thoughts barely reach my brain. Somehow I find protection in my wallet and get the prophylactic on. Her pussy's wet. I can tell just by her scent, but I rub the head of my sheathed cock over her entrance. When I find it as juicy as expected, I thrust in.

She cries out, arching her breasts toward the ceiling.

"Annabel," I croak. I grip her thighs, holding her captive for my rough assault. If I could hold back, I would, but it's impossible. Everything I learned in my youth about being a skilled and tender lover is lost.

I'm the monster now, the beast. All I can do is rut like a wild animal.

Unbelievably, Annabel doesn't seem to mind. In fact, she's as frenzied as I am, crying out, fisting the bedcovers. I pick up her wrists and pin them over her head. She rolls her hips, moans wantonly. I pound so hard, her ass bounces on the bed, and the bed itself skids across the room until it hits the far wall.

"Gotta fuck you. Gotta fuck you so hard," I rumble.

"Yes, yes, Charlie."

I love the way she gives herself to me. The same way she did back in her apartment—with total abandon, total willingness. It feeds me, makes my drive to take her even stronger.

And I want it all. Some base instinct in me, the beast in me, wants to claim every part of her body, every orifice.

I pull out and flip her over, giving her ass a hard slap.

"Oh!" Her cry of surprise only makes my throbbing dick harder. There's lubricant in the bedside table drawer. I bought it last week when I jacked off twenty times thinking about my beautiful handler. I lunge for it, squeeze an ample amount over my cock.

My brain's telling me no. Trying to put on the brakes, but the wolf won't listen. He wants to claim. Needs to claim. He's dying to claim. And for some reason, taking her ass is important. The final fucking frontier.

I squeeze some over her anus, she jerks, and looks over her shoulder at me. I can tell by her wide eyes she's an anal virgin. I should stop now. Ask permission. Talk about it.

I try to speak, but the words come out as gibberish. All I can decipher is her name. And there seems to be the attempt at a question. Something like "Ineedtofuckyourass-canIfuckit Annabel?"

I'm already rubbing my thumb over her anus, massaging the tight ring of muscles open.

"Charlie?" There's fear in her voice—fear I should heed.

Instead, I'm making her promises. "I'll make it good, sweetheart. I promise I'll make it good."

My thumb enters her, and she moans, relaxes for me.

"Good girl. Let me in." I fuck her with my thumb until the muscles have loosened and stretched, and she's used to the sensation. Then I line my lubed cock up with her back pucker. "That's it, baby. Take my cock."

She whines a bit but lets me in, and I don't know how,

but I manage to go slow, slow, slow. I fill and stretch her, easing in, inch by inch.

"Fucking Christ, Annabel. Christ!" I'm lost—in awe of her trust, her total allowance.

She wriggles her hand under her hips, and I move to help her, covering her fingers with my own, rubbing her clit as I pump into her ass.

"Charlie... Charlie. Oh, Charlie."

"That's it, sweet girl. You're taking me so well."

Her pussy is beyond juicy. It's the wettest, most swollen piece of heaven I've ever felt. I flick my finger against her clit as I claim her ass.

My balls draw up tight, thighs start to quake.

"Yes, Annabel. Fuck, yes." I shove three fingers in her pussy as I come, hoping to give as good as I got. Her muscles flutter against them, so I know she came too.

I'm delirious. Grateful and satisfied and still crazed for her all at once. I pull out, but I haven't had enough.

Annabel

CHARLIE TURNS me around again and fists the hair at the top of my head. He uses it to tip my chin up and kisses me thoroughly. No, it's less a kiss and more a devouring. He takes my mouth, drags his lips along my jaw, down my neck. He bites my shoulder.

"Fuck, Annabel. I've never felt this way with anyone before."

Tears pop into my eyes at that. The rough admission

seems so out of character for the secret agent who never shows his cards.

I've never felt this way with anyone before either. I've never even experience one-tenth of this much passion. Charlie is rough but so self-assured. Yeah, I was scared to try anal, but I trusted him. He's good at everything he does. And he was definitely expert in that respect.

My pussy and anus throb a bit, but it a delicious, well-used sort of way. I certainly received as much pleasure as he took—maybe more.

He pulls back and just stares down at me, still holding me captive by the hair. I love being at his mercy—knowing his body is a trained weapon, that he's capable of subduing me in a myriad of ways. One yank and he could snap my neck.

But he won't.

He's here to protect me. He may have just given up his job for me. Hell, his life is probably forfeit now.

That's why I wanted to thank him with the blowjob while Sarah and Grady are out. It's not because I couldn't stop thinking about the frenzied way he took me yesterday up against the wall or because I needed him to help me forget again.

"Funny," I touch his cheek, "your eyes look blue right now."

He freezes for a moment, then blinks and retreats, backing off me. "Do they? My father's used to change, too." His voice sounds strange. But then he turns back to me and scoops me off the bed.

He's impossibly strong. He carries me like a child to the bathroom where he starts the shower. "Let me clean you up." His eyes are back to green.

I stand and watch him undress, dragging my lower lip

through my teeth when I catch sight of his ribbed abdominals, the hard pecs. He's covered in scars—knife wounds, bullet holes, burn marks—each one only adds to the stark beauty of his warrior body. He disposes of the condom in the trash and kicks off his boxer briefs.

And—oh lord—his cock still stands at attention for me. How is that even possible?

He tests the water temperature. I'm standing here, mute, the whole time. I must be in a daze from the orgasm—a satisfaction stupor.

He nudges me gently inside, then follows behind me. He picks up the bar of soap and rolls it between his hands, then strokes my body with it. His hands coast down my arms, up my sides, over my breasts.

The tenderness that was absent during sex stuns me now. He's almost reverent—like he's worshipping at the temple of my body or the altar of love.

No, not love.

I need to stop thinking that way. We've had incredible sex because we're under enormous stress. Under normal circumstances, I never would get involved with someone from the organization.

But that's not true, either. If I'd known what it was like to be taken hard by Charlie Dune, I would've been begging him for it every single meet up we had. I'm almost sorry now for all the missed opportunities.

Charlie turns me in the water, washes the crack of my ass, between my legs, down my thighs. He strokes me with reverence like he's savoring the sensation of my skin, the water, the slide of the soap. When he rises, he wraps me in his arms, and we stand under the water.

"You're still shaking, angel."

I am. My body trembles from the sex, my legs still barely

hold me up. But now, as the high of the orgasm washes away with the soap, reality sets back in.

"I'm afraid, Charlie."

He smooths the wet tendrils of hair back from my face, brings his forehead right up to mine.

"I won't let anything happen to you or your family. I promise you that, Annabel."

I believe him because Charlie Dune is a force of nature. Nothing could stop him from achieving a target.

"Thank you," I whisper. "I can't thank you enough. This is way more than what I did for you."

He kisses me, lips moving over mine, sultry and soft. "We're in this together now. No going back. I'm going to keep you safe. Okay?"

I nod mutely.

The water turns cold, and he turns it off and steps out first. His ass is a work of art—muscled buns leading down to thick, strong thighs. He wraps me in a towel and pulls me in for another kiss.

"Let's get dressed, and we'll talk strategy."

I'm comforted by the word *strategy*. It's something my analytical mind can get busy on besides the worry gnawing me apart.

Charlie

"You okay with doing this?" I ask as Annabel seats herself in front of the laptop and cracks her knuckles. She told me she thought of a way to hack the CIA that would be untraceable.

"Hacking our employer? We're not going to hurt anything. If there's a cover-up here, I wanna know."

Her lower lip juts out a little. My brave, beautiful girl.

Except she's not mine. I can't have her, can't keep her. I clear my throat.

"All right. Show me your father's file."

"Your wish is my command." She quirks a pert little grin. "You really like giving orders, don't you?"

"You have no idea," I murmur, distracted by her fingers dancing over the keyboard, slender and graceful. If I told her to turn around and touch me instead, they'd feel so...

"Charlie?"

I search my memory for the echo of what she just said. "No, I haven't had much dealing with Agent Tentrite." I pace to the window and look out, getting some distance between us. It doesn't work. Her sweet scent teases my nose until I can envision her stretched out on the bed. The rapid clicks on the keyboard remind me again of her small hands caressing my—Damn, I'm used to being attracted to my lovely, aloof handler, but this is beyond attraction. I'm obsessed. I fear it has too much to do with the monster I'm becoming.

"All this happened after I made inquiries about my father. There's a bunch of redacted data in his file. I've been trying to hack it with a higher-level clearance, but—" Her voice cuts off abruptly.

"What?" I stride to her side. "What is it?"

"It's not here."

"You sure? Maybe they moved it."

"No, I'm in the code. The file is here, but the info... it's gone."

I curse.

"Wiped. All of it."

"Who did it, can you tell?"

"No, but I'm about to find out." Her voice hardens.

I stay at her side will she probes. Her brows knit, and her lips move a little as she focuses on the screen. The minutes stretch, but I don't move, don't speak, don't break her concentration. After we showered she put on a light t-shirt, loose enough so if I edge forward I can see straight down the collar to the lovely slope of her—

Cursing myself, I make my eyes fix on the pine paneling of the cabin wall. My cock is at attention, fighting to punch out of my pants. This is ridiculous. I've never been this out of control. But now I'm a prisoner of my own... baser nature.

In any case, it's a good thing I never slept with Annabel before now. I'd be absolutely useless in the field.

"Got ya," Annabel whispers in satisfaction.

"Who?" I bend over her, resisting the urge to nuzzle her hair. The screen is a mess of glowing code.

"Last access was early this morning. Zero three hundred hours." She curses. "I should've hacked it last night."

"It's all right. You were tired." I squeeze her shoulder. "We had no way of knowing someone was going to log in to your dad's file at three in the morning."

"The user signed in and spent a few minutes in here before wiping it," Annabel continues, her voice a bit shaky. This isn't just another mission for her. This is personal. "But they couldn't completely delete the file with their access clearance. I traced the user profile to a dud email account. It's a fake name, but I got the IP address and—" she rattles off a bunch of technical steps that leaves my head spinning.

"English please."

"Sorry." She gives a wan smile. "I forget you don't speak nerd."

"You speak it well enough for the both of us. Who wiped the file, Annabel?"

She turns a little pale but says in a clear, strong voice, "Agent Tentrite."

Annabel

"THIS IS JUST like when we were teenagers." I grin up at Sarah, who scowls because I moved. She has a pair of scissors in one hand and a lock of my hair in the other, and she's thinning the edges like a professional hairstylist.

I've bleached my hair to a respectable housewife blond, and now, Sarah's giving me a shoulder-length layered 'do. "Remember when you shaved the side of my head and dyed the bangs purple?"

Sarah laughs. "We were so sure mom would freak out, but she didn't say a word."

"Yeah, I think she actually got the last laugh on that one."

We both sober, grief from our mother's death still present after two years.

My sister sifts her fingers through my hair. "This is pretty extreme."

"You don't think it looks good?"

"No... it's just hard to think of my baby sister dyeing her hair and going undercover."

"It's not that big a deal," I say, even though my stomach is flipping at what Charlie and I are about to do. "I'll be fine."

She sighs. "Don't lie to me. I know it's going to be dangerous. You won't even tell me what it is."

"That's for your protection. Hey," I grab her hand and squeeze. "I'm not lying. I'm going to be careful. Besides, Charlie will be with me. Do you really think he'd let something happen to me?"

Biting her lip, she shakes her head. Already she looks less worried. There's a bit of Charlie hero worship reflected in her eyes.

"So, tell me," Sarah says in a low voice even though we're in the bathroom, and Grady's watching The Incredibles out in the living room. "Did you two have a quickie while we were out for our walk this morning?"

I smile at her in the mirror and waggle my eyebrows. "It wasn't that quick."

She grins back. "It's about time you—"

"Shut up."

She and I both know my dating life is non-existent. My single-parent sister does way better in that department which doesn't say much.

"He's hot."

I shift in my chair, still sore in all the right places from the rough way he took me. "Yeah, definitely."

"So? Is it forbidden?"

"Handler-field agent relationships? I don't know. Probably. Even if it's not, it's highly impractical."

"Because they travel around a lot? Live in high danger?" Sarah uses a star-struck tone like we're talking about a *Mission Impossible* character and not the very real, very sexy Charlie Dune who hopefully can't hear us from the kitchen where he's eating his eighth meal of the day while he makes us fake IDs. He even printed credit cards with our new names. I had no idea such a thing was possible, and I've worked at the agency for ten years.

"I mean, actually, it's probably not forbidden for the field agent. They're allowed to pretty much do anything they want, so long as they complete their missions. But I might be reprimanded. I don't know."

Sarah's lips twist into a knowing grin. "Worth it?"

"So, worth it." I want to tell her all about it—she is my sister, after all—but the thought of Charlie overhearing is too embarrassing. I just make my eyes really round in the mirror and nod my head slowly like I'm in awe.

Sarah smothers a giggle. "So, you're going as Mr. and Mrs. What-was it?"

"Barnard. Brett and Melinda."

"Mindy Barnard," Sarah muses as she bends her knees to get eye level with me and cuts my bangs. "It has a cute ring. When's your birthday?"

"March 13th, 1986."

"Your sign?"

"Um... Pisces. No one is going to ask me that. I'm not using a fake ID to get into a bar."

Sarah shrugs. "You never know. Better safe than sorry."

I roll my eyes, but secretly I'm glad Sarah's enjoying this and not getting overly freaked out.

Charlie appears in the doorway. His eyes lock onto mine, and I swear they turn ice blue again. His nostrils flare. "Fuck," he says, and shakes his head like a dog shaking off water.

"What?"

"You look..."

I tug my hair out of Sarah's grasp. "It's horrible, isn't it?"

"No." His voice sounds strangled. "I loved the red, but..."

He shoves his hands in his pockets. "You look good. Really good."

I cock my head to the side. "You got a thing for blondes?"

"No, I—" He stops. "Not until now, I didn't," he mutters as he literally walks backward, his eyes still glued to mine.

Finally, with another shake of his head, he hits the kitchen.

5

GODDAMN.

It nearly killed me to tell Annabel she had to cut and dye her hair. Especially since I haven't fulfilled my fantasy yet of riding her from behind with a fistful of that dark auburn thickness to hang onto.

But she looks absolutely angelic as a blonde. The deep red played up her personality—she rocked with the large-framed glasses and the dark lipstick. Now she looks like the girl next door. And damn if I don't want to tie her to the bed and fuck her until she weeps for mercy.

I bang around in the kitchen, trying to satisfy my lust with food. I can't seem to eat enough.

After a full spaghetti dinner, I'm still hungry for red meat. I've already eaten the cans of chili in the cupboards. I pull out a container of spaghetti sauce and eat it straight out of the jar. And let me tell you—it has pathetically few chunks of meat for what's advertised.

I can't seem to eat down the heat though. Every day the moon waxes, and I still don't know what will happen when it's full.

I'm restless as hell. I want to be outside, running —hunting.

Either that or I need to be pounding into my lovely handler again. Making her scream my name until all hours of the morning.

But that's not possible.

I rinse the spaghetti jar out and drop my spoon in the sink. "I'm going to go scout around outside," I mutter to Annabel who emerged from the bathroom with her new look. "Don't wait up for me."

"Wait—what? Is that code for something? Where are you really going?"

Damn perceptive agents and their detective skills.

I take off my shirt and watch her eyes track my pecs. "It means I'm going for a run. We've been cooped up here all day, and I won't be able to sleep unless I get some exercise."

"In the dark? Never mind. You probably can see in the dark, too, right?"

If only she knew.

I step outside and strip out of the rest of my clothes behind the cabin. I don't even have to will myself to shift —it's like it happens without me even asking. Which makes me wonder if I'd have been able to stop it if I wanted to.

But thoughts are lost as I take off, loping across the soft pine-scented earth, nose to the ground, looking for a scent to follow.

Time slips. Distance and direction are irrelevant. I find a

scent that sends thrills coursing through my furry body and take off.

An animal. Deer.

Excitement shudders through me even as my brain screams, *Don't kill Bambi.*

Or Bambi's mother. Whatever.

Too late. I lunge. Attack. Rip out its throat.

The rest is too disgusting to relate.

I'm a goddamn monster.

I lose track of time. Of location. Of identity.

The next thing I know, I'm furious, trying to get to something that's mine.

Someone or something is keeping me out.

A closed door.

I snarl, throw my body against the door. The cabin shudders under my weight.

A female's scream tickles a place in my brain. Fear, it signals fear.

But that's not right. Because that's *my* female inside.

Mine.

And I can't... get... in... to claim her.

A sound scrapes nearby—a window cracking. Her scent grows stronger.

Then another sound that tickles my brain—the cocking of a gun.

The monster recedes, and I realize with horror where I am. What I'm doing.

But before I can leave, Annabel fires.

My own whine pierces the air, and I'm leaping away before my brain gives the command.

Trees blur around me as white-hot pain sizzles in my flank.

Then I'm on the ground. Naked.

A man again.

Jesus, fuck. I almost killed them.

I tried to break into the cabin where Annabel, Sarah, and Grady were.

What would've happened if I'd succeeded?

A shudder runs through me.

I don't know how long I lie on the ground, but when I finally drag myself to my feet, I find the bullet wound isn't even bleeding anymore. A lump of cold metal appears to be right at the surface. I squeeze the edges of the wound between two fingers, and the bullet pops out.

Huh.

So, healing is a wolf superpower. I rub my forehead as I trudge back in the direction of the cabin. Who knows how far I've run away from it.

If Annabel and her sister didn't still need me, I'd keep right on running, away from civilization and anywhere else I'd do harm.

I'm going to have to figure out a way to lock myself up at night. Keep far away from people.

And I'd better get this damn mission wrapped up before the moon is full. I need to get the hell away from Annabel. Forever.

I'm a danger to her.

I just thank God she knows her way around a pistol. If I threaten her again, she can take me down.

Permanently.

Annabel

I GRIP the gun with shaking fingers. The CIA couldn't send a wolf to get me. This isn't a sci-fi film. It was just some enormous, rabid wolf that must've smelled food inside and wanted in.

Still, my heart won't stop thumping against my ribs, the sound of the gunfire and the wolf's yelp echoing in my ears.

And Charlie's still out there.

But he'd know what to do. He's that kind of guy. He'll have a weapon on him, or he'll make one out of a branch or rock. He's a trained assassin, for God's sake. I don't need to worry about him.

As if I could stop though.

Sarah finally gets Grady to sleep, and I'm starting to freak out about Charlie's long absence and the giant rabid wolf. I pick up the gun.

"Maybe I should go out there."

"Are you crazy?" Sarah snaps. "That's how every movie character gets killed."

"What if Charlie needs help?"

"Then we'd hear something. Right now, I don't hear anything—man or wolf. So, just—"

The door swings open to reveal Charlie's figure, head bent to investigate the deep gauges in the door from the wolf's claws.

"Oh thank God!" I rush for him.

He stiffens, and I try to put on the brakes. I'm probably acting too much like a girlfriend as if we have a relationship. Worrying for his safety probably crossed all kinds of boundaries with him.

I draw up short in front of him, and he deftly relieves me of the gun that's still in my hand.

"What's going on?"

"Did you hear the gunfire?"

Charlie's brows slam down. He shuts the door and locks it.

"What gunfire?" he barks.

"A giant, rabid wolf was trying to get in the cabin. That's what you see there on the door. I shot him, but he's probably still out there. I was afraid he'd attack you."

Charlie's mouth pulls down in a grim line. "Never worry about me. Are you three safe?"

When I nod, he steps forward. "I'm sorry I wasn't here to protect you."

He pulls me into the embrace I was craving, and even though I was resolved to keep my emotional distance, I immediately melt into him. His strong arms are like the safety bars on this rollercoaster ride we're on. The one that only grows more frightening every minute it continues.

When he pulls away, he has that blank expression on his face. His game face. I'm not sure what it means. "Where did you hit the wolf, Annabel?"

"In the hip," I admit. "Left flank."

"Is that what you aimed for?"

I go still. It's a strange question, almost like he knew what happened back there. A prickle of defensiveness stiffens my spine. "Yes."

I can hear my basic training arms instructor shouting at me now. *Aim to kill or don't shoot at all. This isn't television. Don't shoot their kneecaps when your life's at stake. If you're not willing to kill, don't draw your weapon.*

I lift my chin and match Charlie's stare. I don't need a lecture from him.

"You know what I'm going to say," he says quietly, and I swear I hear sympathy in his voice.

I nod.

He touches my face, runs his thumb along my cheekbone. "I'm glad you can handle yourself with a gun," is all he murmurs, sparing me a lecture.

I flash him a grateful look.

"Go on, get some sleep. We'll leave before dawn."

I'm disappointed even though we can't sleep together, and there's nothing more to say. He cups my nape and pulls me into him to drop a kiss on my forehead.

I smile faintly at the gesture.

Don't get used to it.

This adventure with Charlie Dune is a one-off. If I get out of this alive, we'll be parting when it's over.

Still, I like the way he makes me feel.

The safety and protection his presence means to me.

No, it's so much more than that. It's raw attraction, fascination with his prowess—both mental and physical—and a genuine connection.

But that still doesn't mean this can go anywhere.

6

C*harlie*

ANNABEL'S BURNER phone rings on our way down the mountain. She looks at the screen, then meets my inquiring gaze. "Washington, D.C. It might be Senator Flack."

"Answer it."

Her hands tremble a bit as she slides the phone on. "Agent Gray speaking."

"Annabel, hi. This is Senator Flack returning your call." With my new and improved hearing, there's no conversation I can't eavesdrop on—including Annabel and her sister's yesterday about me. The senator sounds warm and friendly, almost grandfatherly.

"Senator, thank you for calling me back. I know you were director of the CIA when my father died, and I remember you coming to the funeral."

"Yes, that's true. Your father was a friend of mine, Annabel. He was employed as a covert agent under me."

"Can you tell me what his mission was when he died?"

Senator Flack goes quiet for a moment. "You know I can't do that, Annabel. You should know better than to ask. It's way above your security clearance."

"Yes, I understand that. I do. I just wanted to know... well, never mind. You're right. I shouldn't ask."

"Annabel, your father died a hero. He served his country. It makes no difference whether he did it for the Marines or the CIA."

"Right. Thank you, sir. That means a lot."

The Senator goes on a bit about keeping America strong against our enemies, one of his main platforms when he runs for office. It's a bunch of political hot air, but he the way he preaches it is compelling.

"Annabel, are you at Langley?"

"No, Senator, I'm in California."

"Oh, that's too bad. I would say we could have lunch sometime if you want. I can share some old stories about your dad."

She glances at me, and I nod—meeting with this guy could give us more information. "Actually, I'm headed to the Capitol today. I'd love to have lunch. Would tomorrow work?"

"Yes, yes that would work nicely," he booms. "Call me tomorrow morning, and I'll give you a location."

"Sounds great, thanks." She hangs up. "Did you get all that?" she asks me.

I nod. I may have a big secret to keep from her, but I won't lie if I don't have to. She might just assume my excellent hearing is part of my field agent super skills. "It doesn't sound like he knows."

"Yeah," she gnaws her lip. "But he was the director the CIA at the time. Is it possible there was a cover-up—kept from him?"

"I don't know, but I'm sure we can get the answers if we keep digging. Is that what you want?" I notice she backed down with Flack. Maybe she's ready to drop this.

She nods, still looking distant.

I take my right hand off the wheel and grab hers. "Hey, whatever happens, it's gonna be okay. We'll find the whole story about your dad."

"That's what I'm afraid of."

"Don't be afraid of the truth. You're strong. You can handle it."

"Thanks, Charlie," she whispers. Fuck, but I love my name on her lips.

So does my cock. It perks up, ready to stand at attention. *Down, boy. Now is not the time.*

"So," I say a bit louder to get her attention and my own thoughts under control. "Are you ready for this?"

"Absolutely," she almost giggles, but it's a nervous laugh. I can smell the fear radiating off her thanks to my new and improved mutant senses.

She's not a field agent. Hell, she pulled her shot when my wolf was going to break down the door and kill her family. I'm not used to second-guessing my decisions, but I'm doing so now.

"I could go in alone. You don't have to come with me."

She rolls her eyes. "I need access to Tentrite's office and see for myself what she's hiding. Besides, I wouldn't let you do this alone. I hate that I roped you into all of this, but here we are. We're a team. For better or for worse."

For better or for worse. I hope it doesn't come to that. Still, the scent of her fear plays on my ingrained need to protect her. Shelter her.

"It's going to be near impossible." I have a plan that will get us in under the radar, but still...

"I love a challenge." Her voice is steady, her gaze resolute. She may be scared, but there's no way I'm talking her out of this.

The defiant gleam in her eyes combined with the heady anticipation of danger makes my cock strain its confines. The sooner this is over, the sooner I can have her spread out under me.

"Get ready." I shift the car gears and pull onto the main road. "We're gonna break into the CIA."

Annabel

CHARLIE DUNE IS A MADMAN. That's all I can conclude. Who breaks into the CIA? *Holy shit, I'm about to break into the freaking CIA!*

When we realized Agent Tentrite wiped my dad's file, I was ready to call the trail a dead end.

"Not so fast," Charlie said. "There are two reasons Tentrite would meddle. The first is if she was involved in your dad's career."

"That wouldn't make sense, she wasn't around at the time of his service."

"So, it's the second reason. Someone ordered her to do it."

"Who?"

"That's what we have to find out." A search through Tentrite's file didn't reveal any connection to my dad at all.

"That's the first reason ruled out completely," Charlie muttered. *"Now we work on the second."*

Which brought us to the present moment.

"So, what are we going to do?" I ask, trying not to squirm in my seat of the rental car. We're waiting in a parking lot of a shopping mall.

"Break into your boss's office. Look for evidence of who ordered her to terminate your dad's file."

"I know that." The thought of committing an act of espionage against my own employer has been the only thing on my mind since Charlie first suggested it. "I meant *how* are we going to do it?"

"Trust me." Charlie gets out of the car as a nondescript van pulls up next to us. An older man in a navy jumpsuit exits the driver seat.

"Hey, Charlie." The man's face breaks into a grin.

"Otis." Charlie pumps the man's hand. "Good to see you."

"Where you been?"

"Here and there. You know how it is."

"I do, I do. Hello, there," Otis greets me as I approach.

Charlie puts his arm around my shoulders. "This is my friend. Her father used to work in the service."

"Pleasure, pleasure." Otis bobs his head. I note that Charlie doesn't use my name.

"Did you get my message?" Charlie asks.

"I did. I think it'll work. I usually have a crew working that floor tonight, anyway."

"What?" I gasp. How often had this guy broken in?

They chuckle at my shocked expression. "Otis works there," Charlie says as Otis opens the side of the van door and pulls out matching overalls.

"Today," Otis says, "you do too."

"THIS FEELS LIKE A LONG GAME," I whisper to Charlie as we walk down a corridor. We're in the basement of the CIA, having infiltrated as janitors. Not the scale-and-rappel *Mission Impossible* kind of action I was expecting—kinda anti-climactic, really—but certainly effective.

"It pays to be nice to people," he whispers back and holds a door open for me. I push a janitor's cart. We pass a guy in a suit, headed home after a long night. His eyes skim past our uniforms and cleaning supplies like we're invisible.

I wait until we're in the elevator to turn to him. "Seriously, did you know you'd be doing this someday?"

He shrugs. "It seemed like a possibility."

I bug my eyes out at him.

"Otis is a friend," he explains. "He owes me a few favors."

"And he just happens to work at the CIA?"

"Used to be in the field. He got injured and didn't want to sit and collect disability checks."

Come to think of it, I noticed Otis walked with a slight limp. "So, he became a janitor?"

"He likes to keep an eye on things. Make sure the higher-ups are doing the right thing by their spies. Sometimes, the desk jockeys aren't as loyal to us in the field as they should be. Otis watches the watchers." Charlie holds a finger to his lips. "Don't tell my handler."

I stare at him a moment, trying to figure out what else I don't know about Dune the soldier-spy. What other interesting friends he has.

"What?" he murmurs.

"You're different than I thought." He stiffens slightly, so I add, "Not in a bad way. I just remember when I first met you, I thought you were an arrogant hot-shot. I never guessed you'd be willing to help me this far. Or have a back-door into the CIA."

"I have a little depth." He tucks a strand of hair behind my ear. "And I'm discerning about where my loyalties should lie." His gaze heats the space between us, and I nod, swallowing. In this close space, there's suddenly not a lot of air.

The elevator opens on the floor of Tentrite's office, and Charlie takes over, pushing the cart down the hallway. He goes right up to Tentrite's door and opens it with Otis' key.

"Anything out of place?" Charlie asks.

I look around, pulse jumping. I've been in here before for routine meetings, but this is totally illicit. We've been threatened, chased, shot at. If I get caught in here, there's a good chance the government will make me disappear—permanently. No, maybe I'm over-analyzing.

"What's the penalty for this, do you think?"

"I think we better get through our search and leave before someone catches us and we find out." He gives me a gentle push.

Yeah, I wasn't overanalyzing.

We search in silence, wearing gloves. Fortunately, it fits in with the janitor act. I dust a little as I go, just to make our cover credible. Tentrite has every award she ever won on display. A few statues litter her bookshelves—trophies from a volleyball championship in college. I'm surprised she doesn't have ones from middle and high school as well. I dust while rolling my eyes.

Charlie searches the desk. When I pass close to him, he's meddling with the phone.

"You're bugging the phone?"

"Yeah." He shows me the tiny patch. "New issue to field agents."

"Won't she recognize it?"

"Only if she thinks to look. Which hopefully won't happen for a few days. That's all we need." He sounds so confident I believe him.

"What about her files?"

"Nothing of note." His face changes. "Someone's coming. Get in position."

Heart pounding, I grab a window wand and a bottle of cleaner. Dune ducks behind the desk—I guess it would seem weird to have two janitors in one office. I keep my face turned to the glass. My hands shake so hard, I almost drop the bottle—twice—before spritzing the window. The wiper clatters on the glass.

Steady, Annabel. You got this. Is it weird that my inner cheerleader sounds like Charlie?

I listen hard for footsteps and finally hear them down the hall. Charlie must have super spy senses to pick up on such a slight noise. I guess that's why he's a field agent and I'm not.

I tune everything out and focus on being the best one-night janitor ever. I spray more cleanser and get into a rhythm—wipe, wipe, spray, wipe, wipe, spray. It's almost soothing, and it keeps my attention until Charlie stands up.

"All right," he says. "They're gone."

"About time." I let my arms drop, limp with the strain of acting normal. I've been cleaning the same spot on the window over and over. If I had to play janitor much longer, Agent Tentrite would be walking in tomorrow to a hole in her window. "Who are all these weirdos working late?"

"You're one to talk," Charlie snorts as he continues searching the file cabinet. "When was the last time you took a vacation?"

I feel a pang remembering how many times I talked

about doing Disneyland with Sarah and Grady but never really planned anything. No, I haven't done anything fun since... I don't know. Elementary school?

I force a smile. "This week actually. I'll have you know I had a relaxing stay in a cabin in the woods."

"Really? Sounds creepy."

I have a snappy comment ready when I remember the giant wolf that tried to get inside. I swallow, my stomach flip-flopping in a way that has nothing to do with the fact that I'm rifling through the papers on my boss's desk.

"It wasn't so bad. Except for this annoying guy who kept hanging around while I was trying to relax." I glance over and see a shadow of a smile on Charlie's face.

"Annoying guy? Could be trouble."

"I think I can handle him."

"I think he won't know what hit him."

I turn back to my search. My pulse is high, my blood humming with happiness. Adrenaline has hit, and I'm not nervous anymore. Just... giddy.

Either that or I'm falling in love with Charlie, the super spy.

He crouches and opens a file cabinet door. "Bingo. Found the safe."

I peer over his shoulder at the black box that looks like it means business. "Can you crack it?"

"Fingerprint and voice recognition," he indicates the fingerprint pad, and I slump.

"Damn."

"Hang on. Don't give up yet," he murmurs and reaches into his overalls. "Otis gave us a few gifts." He pulls a black cloth over his finger and shows me the pad on the end.

"Her fingerprint?"

"Lifted fresh this morning." He presses his cloth covered finger down on the pad and waits for the beep before lifting the finger to his lips to keep me quiet. His left hand produces another long and slender silver device. When he hits the button, Agent Tentrite's voice states her full name clearly.

I hold my breath until the safe clicks open.

"Jackpot," Charlie mutters. He pulls files out by the handful, setting some aside, giving the rest to me.

In silence, we page through everything. Charlie stops me once or twice, closing the cabinet door when he thinks he hears someone coming. I obey even though I never hear a thing. He really does have super spy senses.

The clock above our heads ticks on as we sift through the files. I hand each one back as I'm done with it, and Charlie replaces it carefully in the safe. Leave it to him to know exactly how it was organized.

His breath catches for a second, and I raise my head. "Find something?"

"Nope."

Drat. "I guess it's too much to expect a file marked *Conspiracy, Do Not Read*."

Charlie's lips quirk. "That'd be convenient. Somehow I think your boss is more circumspect."

But then I see one file stuffed inside another file. My heart quickens, fingers tremble as I yank it out. My gasp makes Charlie turn.

"It's my dad's," I confirm. I want to stuff it in our janitor trash can, run to a better lit room and read it.

"Here," Charlie grabs the contents of another file and switches them with my dad's.

"Will that fool her?"

"With a little luck." Charlie tosses the file into the trash can and hands the trash bag to me. "A few days is all we need. Come on." We slip out of the office.

"Hey," a male voice booms. A guy in a rumpled suit and prematurely wrinkled face walks toward us with squeaky shoes.

I give a little shriek and knock the mop off the cart. "Oh! Um, what?"

"Since when do janitors work in pairs?"

Charlie's body language changes to slumpy. He gives his nose a swipe with the back of his hand. "I'm trainin' her." His voice inflection is totally different—like he's bored and belligerent at once. "Otis didn't have time."

The guy gives us both a thorough look, one that has my stomach sinking to my shoes. Even if we get away in this moment, he's going to remember both our faces. It will be simple to identify us.

"I don't mind the training. Makes the job go faster. Working alone can get boring, you know." Charlie rearranges his balls through his thick uniform and affects a gross nose sniff.

Disgust shows on the agent's face. "Right. Well, get back to it, then."

I purposely knock the mop over again, like I'm Clumserella and hurry to put it back on the cart. "Okay, where to now?"

Charlie lifts his chin at the next office over, and I wait for him to open it. We both go in, and he shuts the door. I stare at him with wide eyes.

He holds up a finger, watching the guy's back retreat onto the elevator. As soon as it closes, we both exhale. Or maybe I exhale loud enough for both of us, I'm not sure.

"That was close. Do you think he's suspicious?"

Charlie opens the door. "I don't know. Let's not stick around to find out." He hustles me away.

I'm sure we're going straight down to the parking lot, but Charlie takes the elevator upstairs, to another floor.

"Where are you going?" I follow him down the dark hall, biting my cheek, so I don't complain about his excellent night vision. I can barely see until he stops in front of an office and goes in. "Oh no. Are you serious?"

The nameplate reads *Director Edward Scape*.

"Charlie," I hiss as he moves around the murky shadows. "You can't bug the Director's office."

Before I know it, he's out. His kiss brushes my temple as he passes.

"Just did," he murmurs.

We're halfway to the elevator when it dings. Before the doors open, Charlie presses me up against a door and kisses the hell out of me. I push at him a little, realizing someone is coming down the hall toward us. Then Charlie's tongue sweeps into my mouth, and I'm lost—lost, whimpering, and pressing against him as his length hardens against my thigh—

The lights cut on and I jump. Charlie releases my lips but keeps his hands on me, angling his body to block most of mine from the slick, suited security man standing nearby with an eyebrow raised.

Charlie flashes a charming smile. "Sorry, mate. Otis sent us on an errand and..." He glances back at me and heat shoots through my body, warming my cheeks. "I saw an opportunity and took it. Just got carried away."

"Can I see some ID?"

Oh holy hell.

Charlie whips out a badge with his picture and some other guy's name and flashes it. While the guy's looking at it,

Charlie does some sleight of hand and produces one for me, too.

I don't breathe. Not one little wisp of air.

"You two need to move along, now," the security man says. His brows are stern, but he looks like he's fighting a smile. "Have a good night."

Charlie cuts a suggestive glance at me. "I'll try." They share a little man-to-man smirk, and the guy walks away.

At that moment, I'm ready to jump Charlie's bones.

Sexy super agent man—it turns me on to see how cool he is under all different circumstances.

Charlie

WE'RE ALMOST to the elevator when I realize I didn't completely shut the Director's door. The elevator is taking its sweet time coming up for us. It's almost at our floor when the security guard sees the Director's door, then glances back at us. He hesitates as if questioning his instincts. Two janitors, he's never seen before, on a secure floor, and we only cleaned one office before leaving. He's putting the pieces together. I see the moment we're made.

"Hey," the guy turns, drawing his gun at the same time. "Stop right there."

Wide-eyed, Annabel raises her hands.

"Something wrong, man?" I ask, feigning surprise. He wouldn't have a gun on us if he didn't suspect something.

"Stay there," he orders. "I'm going to check something." Gun still trained on us, he pulls out a walkie-talkie. I can't let him call this in.

I push Annabel behind the janitor cart.

"Freeze," the guard shouts and drops the walkie-talkie.

Before he shoots, I'm down the hall. I grab his shooting arm just as the gun cracks.

Damn. Pain reverberates through my head—super sensitive hearing reacting to the gunshot. Behind the cart, Annabel squeals.

"Stay down," I tell her, in between flipping the man over onto the ground, grabbing his gun, and breaking his arm with a crack.

The elevator dings. I can't risk the doors opening, and someone sees this scene.

I'm back at Annabel's side before the guy I hit slumps to the ground—lightning fast moves, another gift of the monster.

"This way." I grab her hand and walk down the hall. The guy I hit is out—cracked his head on the floor when I flipped him. Otherwise, he would've screamed when I broke his bone. I wrap my untucked shirt around my hand to open the door and usher her into the stairwell. "Come on."

We hurry down the stairs. I keep my hand on Annabel, steadying her as I reach for my comms unit.

"Otis," my friend answers.

"We've been made. Shots fired. Call the police."

"Roger." Otis sounds calm.

Annabel wobbles and I scoop her up, increasing my speed. I'm tempted to just stand on the railing and jump down few remaining stories. With my newfound strength, I'd probably be fine.

I resist the urge, and when I reach the bottom, I set her down.

"That man," Annabel whispers. "Is he dead?"

I check my memory—the guy's chest rose and fell as we left. "He'll be fine."

"I've never seen anybody move so fast." She sounds so shaky, I reach out to steady her, then hesitate. She doesn't though, just clings to me. She doesn't know about the monster, but that might not last for long. It's getting harder and harder for me to hide.

"Sorry."

"What for? You saved my life." She grimaces. "I guess no one told that guy if he shoots first, he can't ask questions later."

I say nothing, just hold her. After a moment, she steps away on her own. My lungs are full of her rich scent. She smells sweet, like candy. The fear in her has faded—replaced by one strong overriding emotion—desire.

"Is it wrong that I'm totally turned on right now?" she asks with a sparkle in her eyes.

"Adrenaline. Common side effect." I'm two seconds away from pushing her up against the wall and fucking her so hard, she can't walk for a week. Judging by her scent, she wouldn't mind.

Just then a thought occurs to me. "Shit, did you grab the file?"

With a grin, Annabel opens her coveralls enough for me to see the bit of paper tucked in her shirt.

"Good girl." Annabel might want to go in the field, but I'm not ready for that. I can't think straight around her, especially if she might be in danger.

"What now?" She looks at me with such trust—as if I'm a hero.

I hope we find the truth about her father soon. Before she finds out what I really am.

I reach past her and push open the door—the one

marked "Emergency Exit Only - Alarm Will Sound." The sound starts right away. After a moment, it mingles with the whine of the cop cars filling the parking lot. Blue and red lights wash over the people evacuating the building.

With an arm around her, I escort her out of the building and blend in with the dismayed and curious staff.

"False alarm?" someone asks.

"Probably just a glitch," another answers. "Stupid sensitive equipment—always malfunctioning."

Out of the corner of my eye, I see Otis pull up in his van and stop right on the edge of the lot, blending with the shadows. In the chaos and confusion, no one even glances at Annabel and me as we amble in that direction and blend away into the night.

7

Annabel

I PULL Charlie's clothes off the second we get in the motel room. His growl is pure animal. He yanks my shirt off, pulls down the straps of my bra, and tosses the contents of my father's file onto the floor. As much as I want to read it, my blood is humming with need. *Here. Safe. Charlie.*

Judging by the hard cock poking me the stomach, Charlie feels the same way. My lips lock onto his as he walks me backward toward the bed, a low rumble coming from his chest the whole time.

I work the button on his pants while he unbuttons his shirt and shucks it.

"Clothes off," he orders as if I'm not working on it. "I need you naked. Now." I love the urgent command of his tone.

In a flash, I'm stripped and on my back, legs spread

wide. Charlie drops to his knees on the floor and pulls my wet pussy against his mouth.

"Do you need me to kiss you here, Annabel?"

I weave my fingers into his hair. "Yes. God, yes."

He licks a long line up my slit, then teases me, sucking and nipping my outer lips in between flicks of my clit with his tongue.

"Charlie," I moan.

"Tell me," he murmurs. "Tell me what you need, baby."

"This. I need this. You. Fuck me, Charlie." It's not like me to be crude, but then again, it's not like me to moan like a wanton love-slut either. But I've never been faced with the perfect specimen of masculine provider before. If we were hunter-gatherers, Charlie Dune would be the guy all the cave-ladies would be throwing off their animal hides bras for.

He's one hundred percent alpha male. The guy you'd want to be on that show *Naked and Afraid* with. The guy you'd want to break into the CIA with.

The guy.

Charlie Dune is him.

And right now, *he's* servicing *me*. Which seems a little backward, considering he's doing me all the favors here.

I sit up—or attempt to which is pretty much impossible because the signal from my brain for *lift your head* came at the same time my pussy told my back to arch and my tits to skim the ceiling. Somehow, I get up on my elbows and choke out, "My turn."

"Oh, honey." Charlie stands up, stripping off his already open pants to reveal the world's hardest boner. He picks up my ankles and draws them together, then lifts them high. "You don't call the shots here." He smacks my ass three times, then bites one cheek.

I squeal, and he yanks quickly away, those ever-attentive eyes scanning my face. They glow clear blue. Beautiful, blue. His eyes have the most interesting habit of changing color in the light.

"Sorry, baby. I'm too rough."

I squirm on the bed, inviting more spanking, more touch.

"No, not too rough. Never too rough. I mean, I like it rough. *Please*, Charlie."

He lays another few hard swats on my ass, then releases my ankles and lifts his chin toward the center of the bed. "Hands and knees."

Oh my God. I freaking love it when he gives orders in bed. I'm more excited than I've ever been in my entire life. Every cell vibrates with anticipation, with the beginnings of pleasure. I need this man like he's my next breath.

I obey him, crawling into position and looking over my shoulder as he rolls a condom over his beautiful cock. He catches my eye and lifts his chin again.

"Move forward. Brace yourself with the headboard."

I love that I'm going to need to brace myself. I crawl forward and lift my hands to grip the iron bed frame.

Charlie swears as he crawls up. "Jesus, baby. You're so beautiful." He strokes his hand up the slope of my arched back and arrives at the back of my head. He curls up a fistful of my hair. "I fucked you as a redhead, I'm going to fuck you as a blonde, and I think you'd better dye this hair dark so I can try you that way, too."

My laugh comes out all throaty and low. "Which do you like best so far?"

He curses again. "That's the problem," he complains. "It's impossible to say. The red was incredible, but you're an angel blonde." He slaps my butt and positions himself behind me. "Spread those knees wider, baby. Show me where you want it."

My eyes roll back in my head with lust. My pussy clenches just from his words. "Right here." I hardly recognize my own voice, it's so husky. "I want it here." I make a stripper move and reach between my legs for one long, slow stroke.

"Uh-uh." Charlie pulls my hand away and slaps my pussy. "You don't get to touch. Not now, baby. Not unless I give you permission."

My belly flutters with the thrills streaking through me.

"You don't come until I give you permission, either." He spanks between my legs again. "You're going to arch your back and take it rough, the way you like it, and you don't get release until I say it's time. Understand?"

I totally don't, but I say, "Yes, sir," anyway. All I know is whatever game he's playing lights up my body like nothing before. And that's saying a lot, considering what we've already done.

Charlie lines the head of his sheathed cock up with my entrance and rubs.

I moan and rock back. He pushes gently and eases in, but I see the tendons standing out in his neck like it's taking all his effort not to slam into me, hard.

I appreciate the care he takes. But I definitely want the gloves off.

"Show me rough," I dare.

He growls—that unnerving animal sound again and thrusts so deep, I think he'll split me open. I lock my elbows and hold firm for it. He stops at the hilt, his growl becoming a purr.

"Good girl," he murmurs.

I whimper and squirm on his cock, trying to get more friction, to convince him to move. He chuckles.

"Don't worry, pretty girl. When I start fucking, you'll feel it."

I'm already feeling it. Believe me. It's just that I'm going to fall down dead right now if he doesn't—

Oof. Yes.

Charlie grips one side of my hips and holds the fistful of hair he took and slams into me. I moan softly.

"Is that what you need, Annabel?"

"Yes... *yes!*" I cry.

He repeats the action, and I shudder as he fills me, the satisfaction exploding to my extremities—my teeth clack shut, my toes curl. He gives four quick pumps, then another hard, deep one.

I hang my head and whimper, the need so strong, I don't know if I can last much longer.

Charlie releases my hair and palms my hips to drill deeper, smacking my ass with his loins as he pumps in and out.

I grow dizzy with pleasure, with desire. He reaches around and rubs my clit.

I choke on a cry.

"Not yet," he warns.

"Please. Oh God, please, Charlie." I'm babbling now. Not even aware of the pleading words shamelessly spilling from my lips. "Please, more. Please, harder. Please, I need to come."

"Not. Yet." It sounds like he's speaking through clenched teeth.

He slams in so hard, I fear I won't be able to keep my arms straight, but then he must realize my dilemma because he wraps one strong arm around my waist to help hold me in place. It brings him closer to me, the thrusts deeper but with less force.

It's delicious. I'm delirious. I'm already soaring, my body celebrating the rightness of being taken by him, my soul reveling in how easy it is to be vulnerable with him, to let down my barriers and let him lead. It's transformational.

Charlie's grip on me tightens. His breath snarls in and out. I sense the shaking of his thighs against mine. He lets out a roar and thrusts in and up, almost lifting me from my knees. He pulls my torso back against his chest and taps my clit with a rapid tap-tap-tap.

I shriek as my internal muscles spasm. I squeeze his cock and pleasure unwinds, ripples through me in waves of pure ecstasy.

Charlie makes a choked sound behind me and pulls out before I finish, which would be more disappointing if I wasn't already on Cloud Nine.

Charlie

OH, Christ. Fuck, fuck, fuck.

I stumble back off the bed and find my way to the bathroom. Something happened when I orgasmed. It was like I was about to shift.

Only different. My canines lengthened, and a sweet taste came into my mouth. My vision is also domed and sharpened like the monster's.

And a terrible desire came over me.

I wanted to sink my teeth into Annabel's flesh.

I throw the condom in the trash and splash water over

my face. The teeth still appear long although they're starting to recede. My irises glimmer a pale blue. Annabel's told me that happened before when we had sex.

What the fuck?

Does a werewolf try to *turn* his mate? Like a bite at full moon makes her a werewolf too? Or do I actually want to kill her? Is the instinct to hunt and to fuck so close, the animal can't tell the difference?

Of all things unholy and wrong.

I am a monster.

Annabel's not safe with me. The full moon is tomorrow, and we're trapped in the city for the night—nowhere for me to run and hunt, to get this aggressive need out of me.

How will I survive the night beside her?

I force a long, deep breath.

Calm the hell down, Charlie.

I've figured my way out of far more difficult situations. I can easily make up an excuse and spend the night in the rental car or get a different motel room.

I return to the room and find Annabel pulling on her clothes with her back to me. Something in her stance—or is it her scent—worries me.

She's hurt. Or embarrassed.

Fuck. I just pulled out and left her. No post-coital cuddle, no thanks, no nothing.

I walk swiftly to her and wrap my arms around her from behind. My lips seek the tender skin behind her ear.

"I'm sorry." Better to own this than to pretend nothing happened. "Being with you is intense for me. I'm not used to experiencing much feeling to anything. I just had to catch my breath for a second."

She turns in my arms. I was right, vulnerability is scrawled across her beautiful face.

"What do you mean?"

I mean I sprouted fangs and almost ripped you apart.

Hell.

"I don't know." I shake my head. "You do something strange to me."

There. That's all true. I'm not going to lie to Annabel if I don't have to.

"I think I should get some air." I release her and pick up my clothes. When I catch the scent of her pain again, I find myself speaking before I can stop it. "Do you want to come with me?"

Great, Charlie. How's that going to work?

But the way her face brightens is worth the difficulty this will cause me. And Lord knows she deserves an outing as much as I do. I pull on my jeans and a worn t-shirt and put on a pair of shoes.

"You hungry?" Because I could eat a freaking T-Rex.

"Yeah."

I pick up the keys to the rental car. "All right, we'll drive to get some food, then find a place to get some fresh air."

She grabs her father's file as we walk out the door. I would tell her to leave it because the goal was to get her mind off this case for a few moments, but I know it won't do any good. She needs to know what's in there. And so do I if I'm going to protect her.

I drive to a diner nearby and park the car. She clutches the file tightly, but I notice she hasn't once cracked it. It's like she's afraid of what she'll find. I can't say I blame her.

Inside I order three hamburgers and a side of bacon. Annabel gets a cobb salad.

"You on the heart-stopper diet?" Annabel teases.

"Yeah. Breaking into the CIA makes me work up an appetite." And the monster inside me needs meat.

"Oh, I thought *I* did that."

If only she knew. "Oh you did, baby. Believe me. You did."

She draws a breath and looks down at the file on the table.

"Go on," I urge.

She opens it, wearing an expression like someone about to face the guillotine. The file is in chronological order with the last mission on the top. I read upside down as she skims the information.

El Salvador.

Agent forwarded his own agenda, acting outside orders from his superiors to incite violence in the villages. His effort to prevent or delay the peace accord failed, and he was killed by locals in a village where he led a massacre on the indigenous people.

Agent Scape cleaned and covered up the incident. Gray's death reported as a Marine casualty on protection detail.

Annabel covers her mouth with her hand while she reads as if to shield her expression from me. She stares at it way too long, but her eyes are still moving. She must be re-reading. Finally, I reach across and pull her hand from her mouth.

"Baby, there's no telling what spin they put on this. Agents make life or death decisions in the field all the time. I'm guessing if your father went off the rails it was for a reason we don't understand. It's hard for me to imagine an intelligent, well-trained agent would just start promoting his own agenda."

Annabel's lips tremble. Tears swim her in beautiful gray eyes. "Do you think he was hired by someone?"

Damn, I don't want to answer this question. I cant my head to the side. "It's possible, yes."

"But who would've hired him?"

"Could've been a special interest group in our country, could've been an international party with a stake in the continued unrest down there."

"Do you think they know, and that's what they're trying to suppress?"

"Well, we know one thing. They don't want this information out there. Now, if it was just about one rogue agent, I'm not sure they'd go to all the trouble of hunting down a notebook. So, yeah, I'd say there's something more to this story. Something not in this file."

"Maybe I shouldn't have kept looking." Annabel blinks hard but doesn't manage to keep the tears back. They track down her face, and she presses her lips together and looks out the window to the parking lot. As if on cue, rain starts to fall.

"Listen, I'm sorry for what you found in there, but I'm telling you, you can't make any judgments about your father or what he did. He's not here to answer for it himself. I would give him the benefit of the doubt." I pick up her hand. "If he produced daughters like you and Sarah, I find it hard to believe he betrayed his country or sold out human lives. I really do."

Annabel's eyes cut away, bitterness flickering over her face. "We were so young when he died, and he was gone a lot before that. Our mother really raised us."

I consider her for a long moment, torn between forever keeping my secret buried and the burning need to ease her pain, to give us common ground.

"We have a lot in common," I finally say. My voice sounds rusty like I hadn't just been talking. "I found out something disturbing about my father, too. It was the case I needed your help with last month."

Her gaze turns sharp, the analyst coming to the fore. "Did he work in the labs?"

"I thought he must've come from the labs. I presumed he'd been part of a government experiment, similar to Nash Armstrong. They shared some similar traits." I shake my head. "But it wasn't what I thought. Not at all. And I found out something... I really didn't want to know."

Now she squeezes my fingers. "I'm sorry."

I clear my throat because I'm entirely unaccustomed to being on the receiving end of anyone's sympathy, but I'm not about to reject anything that comes from my tender handler. Everything about her is too pure, too raw. Too precious.

"I think the important thing is not to make some decision about whether they were good or bad. Or what it says about you. I mean, is it possible to just remember him as your father?"

She releases my fingers, her mouth twisting into a wry grimace. "Now you sound like Director Scape."

Our food arrives, and I have to draw a deep breath to keep from attacking the meat before the plate's even down.

"That's not what I meant," I say between inhaling my burgers. "I don't mean to pretend something or believe in a fairytale. I just mean honor the good memories and withhold judgment on the rest."

Sadness washes over her and a few more tears fall, but she nods. "Yeah, that makes sense. I'll try."

Fuck. It kills me to see her cry. I swallow the last of my burger. Annabel is too distraught to notice I've eaten three days' worth of food in three minutes.

"Come 'ere," I order gruffly, and hold out a hand. She unfolds from her seat and takes shelter in my arms. Her weight in my lap feels so good, so right. She sniffs a little, and I rub her back. "I've got you. Let it out."

Her hands fist in my shirt as she sobs and shudders against me. The monster inside me howls silently, suffering right along with our mate. I keep still, willing the predator within to calmness. If the monster had its way, it'd be on a rampage, killing and hunting in response to our mate's pain. I take big lungfuls of her scent until the need for violence washes away, leaving only Annabel.

When she sits up again, my shirt is wet from her tears. Her eyes are red, and her hair tickles my nose.

She's never looked more beautiful.

I've been running from who I am, my feelings, my pain for most of my life. Ironic that as soon as I accept what I've become, I'm given the greatest gift—a woman to love. A gift I can never accept. She deserves better than me. Another, better man who will treasure her and keep her safe. Will he fight alongside her and comfort her like this? The thought makes my monster rage within the bars of its cage. My muscles tremble with the desire to shift. I grit my teeth and fight it back. It's getting harder to keep control.

The longer I stay with her, the more danger Annabel is in. I better leave soon while the only price she'll pay is a few tears. If I wait too long, the price will be higher. I can't risk the monster hurting her... or worse.

I won't let that happen. I will leave before I hurt Annabel even if it destroys everything we have together. The meat in my stomach sours at the thought, and the monster howls with loss.

Soon, but not tonight. I hold Annabel tighter, and savor this precious moment, knowing everything I've ever wanted in is is in my arms.

≈

Annabel

CHARLIE DRIVES to the National Mall where we walk the moonlit expanse of pathways and grass in front of the Smithsonian Museums.

You would think after wolfing down three hamburgers he'd be moving slow, but it's like he still has energy to burn. I wonder how fast a field agent's metabolism runs. Twice the normal person's? Three times?

Getting to know Charlie Dune as a man, not just a super agent is just as thrilling as watching him in super agent action. Every minute I spend with him deepens my interest, increases my desire.

As terrifying as this whole adventure is, I don't want it to end.

Because I know when it does, Dune and I will have to part ways.

Of course, I don't even know if going back to our old jobs, our old lives is a possibility. Have we both gone too far off the rails to be allowed back in?

Charlie interlaces his fingers between mine like we're a couple—boyfriend-girlfriend. I like it way too much.

"So, what now?" I ask even though this is really my mission. Still, I need Charlie to tell me what to do. I'm in way over my head now.

"What do you want to do, Annabel?"

I knew he'd ask, yet I'm still at a loss. "I don't know," I sigh. "What do you think?"

Charlie's quiet for a long moment. "If it were me? Honestly? I'd keep digging. Something doesn't smell right with all of this. But if you want it to end, if you want to go back to your job and put this chapter behind you, I think we can still negotiate our way back. It's up to you."

I suck in a breath. "I've far exceeded my favor with you."

He stops walking and turns me to face him. "This isn't about the favor. You must know that. I'm here for you, Annabel. There's no way in hell I'm going to let you or the people you love get hurt." He shrugs his muscled shoulders. "It's pretty clear-cut for me. As long as you're still in, I'm in."

My eyes smart, and I blink back tears. How can I stop myself from plunging headfirst into the sea of Charlie? But I have to. This is a man who can't even stay still for an hour in a motel room. He's not going to stick around and do a "relationship" with me. The idea is laughable. It figures I'd fall for a guy just like my dad—the hero who has to be off saving the world instead of doing the picket fence thing.

I feel like a selfish bitch for putting him in danger, but his protection means everything to me.

"Yeah. I'm still in. And Charlie,"—I reach up and touch his face—"Thank you."

His eyes glow for a moment under the moonlight, and he claims my mouth with the same hunger that seems to overtake us every time. Except now we're in public, and he's fucking my mouth with his tongue, grabbing handfuls of my ass in his strong hands.

I laugh and push him away because if I didn't, I swear we'd end up horizontal on the closest park bench.

He blinks his eyes rapidly and sucks in a tortured breath. "Let's get you back to the motel." He loops an arm around my waist and steers me back toward the end of the mall where we parked.

"Me? What about you?"

He hesitates one second too long. "Yeah, me too."

"Where are you going?" I ask sharply.

His smile is both indulgent and rueful. "There's no getting anything past a CIA agent, is there?"

"No. What are you planning?"

He shakes his head. "Nothing. I just haven't walked enough. I need time alone to clear my head. That's all."

Something doesn't quite ring true about his words, and it causes my belly to tighten. What is Charlie keeping from me?

Can I really trust him? Or is this the ultimate play?

But no, he couldn't fake the passion he brings to our sex. Couldn't fake the words that tumble out afterward.

Could he?

Charlie

I HEAD out into the night air, away from Annabel's intoxicating scent. Already I want to claim her again. But even when I do, it's not enough. That desire to bite her—visions of it—keeps rising up.

I fire up a burner phone and dial a Tucson number. It's not like me to call some dude and ask for help. Hell, everyone knows guys don't stop to ask for directions, especially not me. But I don't know what the devil I'm going to do next, and the moon is nearly full. Annabel's life could be in danger.

Tonight.

"Hello?"

"What happens during the full moon?"

The shifter on the other end of the line is silent for a moment. Then he says, "*Dune.*"

"Yeah."

"I wondered if you'd call."

"Answer my question."

"You really still think you're in a position to interrogate me? Try again, asshole." He ends the call.

Okay, I totally deserved that. I am an asshole. The first time I met Jared, I swooped in when local cops raided an illegal cage fight he was in and took over his interrogation. I'd seen his eyes change color the way I remember my father's had. The way Nash's—a guy I knew from Special Forces—had. I thought they were part of a government experiment. Which was only half-correct.

The second time I met Jared, I followed his pack on a rescue mission to Honduras where I saw the pack members change before my own eyes—becoming wolves, lions, a dog, even an owl.

Seeing the impossible somehow activated something in my own biology. My half-shifter status made me vulnerable, and the dormant ability came to the surface. Jared caught me spying and commanded me to change.

And that's how I realized I keep a giant silver wolf pent up inside me.

I dial the number again. "Good evening, Agent Dune." He's mocking me now.

"I'm sorry." It costs me to say it. I can be anything, play any part when I need to for the job, but this is real, and I somehow intuit dominance within a pack means everything. My wolf can't stand me groveling to him. "Please." Again, it costs me. "What happens during the full moon?"

"You'll want to hunt. Eat more red meat. Get out and shift. You have someplace safe you can run?"

I wish to God I was back at my cabin in California. "Not at the moment."

"That's too bad." Then he says sharply, "You have a female with you?"

My body goes tense for whatever he's going to say. "Why?"

"It can make the need worse—if your wolf has chosen her as your mate. You can go moon mad if you don't claim her. Especially during the full moon."

The world around me spins, locks into place—a bad place. "*What's moon mad?*" I already know that's what's happening to me. Why else would I want to tear into Annabel's flesh with my teeth?

"The animal can take over. You shouldn't be without a pack for this. It's your first moon. Where are you, man? Can you get to Tucson? We can help."

"Uh... probably not going to happen. No."

Jared grumbles a bit. "You need me to come to you?"

I'm somewhat shocked by the offer. He would do that for me? I barely know the guy, and the interactions we've had haven't exactly been stellar.

"That's not gonna happen either. But thanks. I appreciate it." I pace around the back of the motel. "What do you mean the animal takes over? Like it tries to hunt? Does it hunt humans?"

"It means you lose your humanity. Yeah, hunting humans is possible. If it happens, you'd have to be put down. That's why I don't want you alone. Where's the female? Is she human?"

"Of course she's fucking human," I snap, then shake my head, as if I can throw off the fear ratcheting up my spine. It's not like me to lose my temper. Or be afraid. But this is Annabel we're talking about.

"Mating a human is a challenge, but it can be done."

"I'm not going to mate her when I could turn savage and kill her on any given full moon."

"Well—"

"Thanks for your help," I cut in. "I'll figure it out on my own."

Like I always have. I end the call. It rings back just as I crush the burner phone under my heel so it can't be traced back to me.

Damn it all to hell.

I'm going to have to get Annabel somewhere safe and very far from me by tomorrow night. I can't risk her being anywhere close to me if the monster takes over.

When I go back to the motel room, Annabel wears a vulnerable-suspicious expression.

"Who did you meet?"

I arch a brow. I'm tempted to dodge the question, but again, the urge to stick closer to the truth with her wins out.

"I had to make a phone call. Not about this mission. About my last one. The personal one. Just trying to wrap things up."

Her expression softens, eyes warm. "The one about your dad?"

My gut twists. "Yeah."

He was a monster, like me.

I want to tell her everything, but she's had enough shock for one day. I don't know how she could absorb this, too. Tomorrow I'll tell her if I have to. To keep her safe.

"I've been doing some more hacking," she says. "On a hunch, I pulled the bank records for Director Scape from 1992. Guess what I found?"

My clever, clever handler. "What?"

"A very large deposit into Scape's account from a

company called American Trade Assets. And several more going back to 1990."

"What is American Trade Assets?"

"That's the interesting part. They're a political action organization primarily interested in promoting American trade interests. Particularly in North and South America."

"So, you think they might have funded a peace destabilization project?"

"That's exactly what I think. Scape was my dad's direct superior. He could've taken the money and sent my dad on the mission."

I hate to ask the next question. "Did you check your dad's bank account?"

She sits up taller. "Yep."

"And?"

"Nothing unusual. Just his regular checks from the Marines."

"He may not have ordered your dad to complete the mission. He might have gone to do it himself, and your dad got in the way," I suggest.

"Yes, that's a possibility, too. Maybe I can find out more from Senator Flack."

I don't like it, but she's probably right. He's a decent lead. "Yes. Call him tomorrow and set up a meet."

I reach out to touch her hair, then pull my hand back. Even with our wild sex earlier, I'm dying to claim her again.

Down boy.

"I'm going to take a shower," I mutter.

A very, very cold shower.

nnabel

"Is this a bad idea?" I ask Charlie for the fifth time since I called Senator Flack on a new burner phone to set up the lunch date.

"I'll have eyes and ears on you at all times. Nothing's going to happen." Charlie straightens the collar of my blouse where the tiny receiver is clipped. The other piece is in my ear, but it's so small, no one would notice even if my hair wasn't covering it.

Oh Lordy, I am never going to pull this off. I am not field agent material that's for sure.

"I could be wanted by the CIA by now. We both could. What if he knows that, and someone's there to arrest me?"

"You already checked the database. Absolutely nothing has been filed about either one of us. Which further confirms there's something fishy to this case."

"How do you mean?"

"I mean, if this were a simple case of you disobeying orders and refusing to call in, it would be right there in your file. It would be mentioned in my file. There would be measures taken—aboveboard measures. There's nothing of the kind. Which means whoever's messing with you isn't aboveboard. Whether it's Tentrite or Director Scape or both, I can't be sure. But maybe this lunch will give you more info."

"Should I tell him what's happening?"

Charlie considers me for a long moment. "I wouldn't, but I don't trust anyone."

I swallow. "You trust me." I don't know why I'm fishing for his reassurance—I don't need to act like a clingy girl-friend, especially at a moment like this. Or maybe it's *because* of this moment. I'm scared. My life is in danger. And Charlie's the only guy in my court.

He palms my hip. "Yeah. I trust you." It seems hard for him to say which makes me think he actually means it.

We take the metro to Union Station. Charlie's doing the "smartly dressed businessman" thing with a suit and tie. He's wearing a pink button down and a tie with shades of gray, purple and red which makes me want to break into applause. Clearly, he's more than man enough to carry off the feminine colors. He does the Bluetooth earpiece talk the entire time, babbling on about orders and shipments. All the while, he's looking around like he sees nothing, like he's only absorbed in his imaginary conversation, but I know he's taking in everything and everyone.

When we exit at Union Station, the place is packed.

Something's going on.

"Oh God," I murmur so Charlie can hear. "It's a freaking

flash mob." People of all ages are joining in, singing and dancing to *Grease Lightning*.

"Perfect," Charlie answers. "Crowd distraction always works in our favor. Just act like you're watching as you slip into the crowd. I'll have eyes on you. Never look back for me."

"Okay." I follow his instructions, smiling at the performers, standing on tiptoe as if I want to see more, all the while weaving through the crowd and out the other side.

There's more havoc in the alleyway beside the station. Roadblocks are set up and crowds standing around. "What's going on here?" I ask someone who's stopped and watching.

"They're filming a movie. I heard it's a new *Terminator,* but I don't think that can be true."

"That's good for me, bad for you. Cross the street and walk where things are clear. I'll blend in with the crowd."

"Copy that." I move across the street, the click of my high heels sounding on the pavement. The restaurant Senator Flack named is in a hotel. I enter the lobby and scan the faces, but don't see the senator's gray head. When I give my name to the hostess, she hands me a piece of paper with a note from the Senator scrawled on it.

"Change of plans," I tell Dune as I walk towards the elevators. "We're meeting in his hotel suite. Fourth floor."

Charlie curses. "What's the room number?"

I tell him, and he's silent a moment. "Everything all right?"

"Yes, but I don't like it. He probably just wants more privacy. And it's not uncommon for politicians to use a hotel suite as a meeting place. Especially when they're on the campaign."

"Campaign?" I ask, threading through a group of tourists waiting for the elevators. It'll be faster to just take the stairs.

"Yeah, haven't you heard? Senator Flack is on the short list of vice presidential candidates. Primaries aren't for another year, but he's gearing up to run."

"Damn," I breathe, pausing at the stairwell door. "Hey, I'm taking the stairs. I might lose signal."

"Go on up. I will be right behind you."

I'M SUDDENLY FLANKED by two men in suits, and the end of a gun pokes my ribs. "Don't say a word."

My breath leaves in a whoosh. Before I realize what's happening, the two guys propel me back toward the stairwell I just exited.

"What's going on? Where are we going?" I narrate for Charlie's benefit.

The gun prods me harder. "I said no talking."

"*No.*" Charlie's sharp voice radiates with danger. "Don't go anywhere with them. If they wanted you dead, you'd already be dead. I'm almost there."

I shove the guy with the gun and duck backward. They both lunge forward and seize my arms. "Help! Fire!" I yell. None of the hotel doors open, but maybe someone will call the police.

The two guys yank me down the first flight of stairs, and I lose my footing. They drag me, banging my foot on the concrete stairs.

"Help!" I scream louder. My voice echoes in the closed space.

"Shut up," one mutters, lifting me clear off my feet as they speed down the next flight of stairs.

Then I hear it—ferocious snarling, unearthly, terrible growls. It's coming from below us.

"What the fuck is that?" The thugs pause on the stair.

"Probably a dog."

The growls grow louder, and I recognize the sound. It's the same one I heard outside the cabin two nights ago.

"Go check it out." One guy yanks me close, and the other sprints down the stairs.

I kick at the guy holding me and get pistol-whipped for the trouble. The world spins for a moment, and I cling to my captor for balance.

The stairwell echoes with a spine-unhinging roar.

That's no dog. The guy holding me comes to the same conclusion because he starts dragging me back up the stairs. I take the chance to fight him. When I fall, he yanks me up by my hair. Stars burst behind my eyes.

Something's leaping up the stairs, a whitish blur. I freeze, then scramble back frantically. I scream when a gun pops multiple times by my head. The blast doesn't hide the sharp ping as a few of the bullets ricochet. I throw my arms over my head and fall to the concrete.

The giant furry thing yowls in pain but keeps coming. Before I can scream again, it leaps past me in a whoosh.

The next thing I know, the stairwell echoes with the guy's screams. I look and immediately regret it. The giant wolf has his jaws clamped on the guy's arm, its weight pinning him down. Blood sprays and my former captor screams—only to be silenced when the wolf lunges forward and...

Adrenaline forces me up off the ground. My shoes go flying, and I'm running down the stairs, ignoring the horrible, meaty sounds behind me.

I don't stick around to be the next meal. I fly down the stairs, barely pausing when I pass the mangled body of my second captor on the way. I slip a little on the smeared blood, and my stomach lurches. I'm too busy running for my life to stop and be sick.

I hit the exit door and end up in an alley. I stagger down it, panting, but nothing follows me. My head throbs, my hair's a mess, my clothes are awry—but I'm alive. I tear off my bloodied pantyhose—they're all torn anyway—and touch my earpiece.

"Charlie?" My voice is shaking. There's no answer. Oh God—he said he was right behind me. Did the wolf get him too? It was the wolf from the cabin—I'm sure of it, but that can only mean one thing.

It's hunting me. Is this some new creepy project of the CIA?

I take off running in bare feet. I don't know if it's stupid or genius, but I rush into the chaos of the movie filming, ducking under the tape and running through the crowd.

"Hey! You can't be in here! Hey!" Voices shout after me, but I don't look back. My feet are getting torn up by the pavement, but I don't stop.

I don't know where to go. Don't know what to do.

Oh God, what just happened? What was that back there? Images I just saw flashback through my head, and I choke, my stomach dry heaving.

"Annabel!" The sound in my ear shocks me into a shriek.

"Charlie! Where are you?"

"Annabel, talk to me. I stole a car. I'll get you in ninety seconds. Where are you?"

There's such authority, that certainty he always exudes, relief rushes over me. "One block south of the movie set, back alley, in a doorway."

"Hang tight."

I hear the screech of tires through the earpiece.

He's coming for me. He protected me, just like he promised. And he'll know what to do.

Charlie

HOLY SHIT. Holy shit. Holy shit.

I just attacked humans. I have human blood in my mouth. I had to wipe it off the front of my chest. The scariest thing—or is it the sanest thing—I wasn't the monster. I was me, just in wolf form. My head was clear. My instincts and reflexes were even faster than normal.

I attacked swiftly, immobilized the attacker, and reached Annabel. I eliminated both threats, despite taking a bullet to the back. Then I had the wherewithal to go back and pick up the comms unit and my clothes with my cell phone, then steal this car and get back in communication with Annabel.

Annabel.

She's probably freaking out. What will I tell her?

I whip down the alleyway just as a bullet sounds. It hits my car.

Damn, I've been detected. A blue Buick is right behind me, and—oh fuck—another car pulls up and blocks the other end of the alley.

I slam on the brakes when I see Annabel. "Get in!"

She looks both ways down the alley, terror making her gray eyes huge. She stinks of fear and vomit. "Where—never mind." She jumps in the car.

I appreciate the hell out of her trust in me.

"Fasten your seatbelt." I throw the car in reverse and back up at full speed, slamming into the Buick. The crunch of metal and shattering glass explodes behind us. I change gear, step on the gas, and zoom forward. I will knock the bastards out of the way, especially with this running start.

"Get the gun out of your purse."

"Oh!" I think she forgot I put it there this morning. My own weapon was lost when I shifted.

A bullet shatters our windshield. "Get down! Return fire if you can."

The driver of the car at the end of the alley moves just in time, apparently not interested in getting crushed. I zoom past and floor it, all four wheels flying when we hit a bump.

"Oh my God, oh my God, oh Jesus," Annabel croaks, but she's got the gun pointed out the window behind us, ready to fire.

They shoot our back windshield, and I shove Annabel's head down again. Three turns and I'm on a major thoroughfare. Traffic is sticky which works in our favor. I work in and out of it, and when I see a big parking garage, I squeal into it.

"Where are you going?"

"We have to get rid of this car." I wind up the garage until I find a spot, and we both jump out. I'm wearing the tatters of my pants, which I have to hang onto, but at least I have my phone, which has the software technology to open any electronically keyed car.

I choose a car and pop the locks. "You drive, I'll shoot." I take the gun from Annabel. "How many bullets left?"

"Um..."

"How many shots did you fire?" I amend my question.

"Three? Four?"

I nod. So, I have at least ten bullets left in the magazine and no sign of our tail. If we're lucky, we lost them.

"Where to?" Annabel backs out.

"Get on the Washington Memorial Highway." I don't have a firm plan, but I think Otis might know where to hide us while we figure out our next move. Keeping my eyes glued to the rearview and side view mirrors, I call my buddy.

"Hm-yello?"

"I need a safehouse that's truly safe." Truly safe means it's hidden even from the CIA.

Otis lets out a curse. He's quiet for a moment, then says, "I have a place for fishing. It's a couple hours away. Is that too far?"

A cabin actually sounds perfect, considering my furry tail and howling at the moon problem. "No, that will work."

"I'll meet you at Rocky Run Park in Arlington to give you the key. Anything else you need?"

"Yeah, weapons, lots of them. And computer equipment. Anything you can spare."

"I'll hook you up. How long until you can meet?"

I grit my teeth. Highway traffic has come to a near stand-still. It's not uncommon on this highway—there must be an accident somewhere ahead, but I don't like it. "Forty-five minutes. Maybe longer."

"I'll be there."

"Thanks, Otis." I end the call and take in the traffic again. It's probably not a police roadblock on a manhunt for us. Then again...

Annabel taps the steering wheel with the tip of her index finger. It's a nervous tell she has—I've seen her do it before.

"Charlie...." The fear in Annabel's scent has me on high alert. "Back at the hotel, I..."

"It's okay, baby," I soothe when her voice dies. Traffic stops entirely, and I take the opportunity to grab her hand

and squeeze. "You did great. I never should've sent you in alone. Someone must have followed us and sent men to grab you." Either Agent Tentrite or Director Flack. Whoever it was, they escalated the situation. As soon as I figured out which one sent the wetwork team, I'd repay them in kind.

"It's not that." She shudders.

"Talk to me," I order as gently as I can.

"I don't know what happened," she almost whispers. "The guys got me in the stairwell—started dragging me down. Then—" Her face whitens. It's killing me not to take her into my arms. "I heard something."

"What, baby?" I ask even though I already know. My body tightens in anticipation.

"It was a growl. An animal—that wolf. I know that sounds crazy, but I swear it was the same wolf from the cabin. It came up the stairs and—" She stops and covers her mouth.

I slide a hand over her back. "It's okay," I murmur over and over even though I feel as sick as she looks. What would've happened if I had been too late? Or if the monster in me took over and continued the hunt? How many people would've died?

With a sharp shake of her head, she recovers. "I'm fine," she says in a way that makes me think she's giving herself a command. "I'm fine. I just need a moment."

I pull my hand away. I don't deserve to touch her. "Take as long as you need."

"I know you think I'm crazy—"

"No, baby," I cut in, but she doesn't seem to hear me.

"—but I swear it was a wolf. It could've been a dog but..." She stares out the window. I wish I could say something to comfort her.

"Annabel..." *I'm the monster you saw.* My tongue is heavy

in my mouth. My stomach twists in disgust at my own cowardice.

"I know you think I'm crazy," she repeats.

"No," I say. "It's possible these guys had... an attack animal with them."

"But it attacked *them*. Not me." Her eyes widen. "Charlie, it rescued me."

My mouth is dry. It doesn't matter how powerful I've become—I can't tell Annabel the truth. I'm not strong enough. I stare at the red brake lights ahead of us and jump when a horn honks angrily nearby.

"I think..." She sounds thoughtful, "I think it tried to help me."

"Whatever it was," my voice rasps, "promise me next time you see it, you'll shoot it down."

"What?"

"Something like that is dangerous. It could've attacked you. If you see it again, gun it down. Promise me." I turn my head so she can't see the desperation in my face.

Her eyebrows knit together. "But—"

"Annabel."

"Fine," she soothes. "I promise."

The brake lights ahead of us blink. Traffic hasn't moved more than an inch in several minutes. Typically for D.C., and yet...

"Something's wrong." My instincts clang in warning, loud and clear. Even before I was a wolf, I knew to trust them. "I have a bad feeling about this, Annabel."

I look around. A motorcyclist leans a foot on the ground a few lanes over in front of us.

"Get out. Leave the car running. Follow me." I exit the car, gun gripped in my hand but held against my leg, so it's semi-hidden. I dart forward through the lanes between cars until I get to the motorcyclist.

Quickly, I lift the gun and tuck it against the guy's ribs, inside the flap of his jacket so the people behind us can't see.

He goes perfectly still but gives us both an up and down look. Annabel's not wearing shoes.

"We need to borrow your bike. Our car is back there, still running."

The motorcyclist eases off the bike without a word. He must recognize the desperation of our situation. Or his.

"Give her the helmet and your jacket."

He scowls but does as I ask him.

"Silver Camry, far left lane."

He walks toward the car, giving us one searching look over his shoulder.

"We'll leave your bike where the police can find it," I tell him.

"You'd better," he calls gruffly back. I almost smile. He reminds me of the wolves in the pack in Tucson, a motorcycle gang of shifters who run cage fights and nightclubs and own the city streets at night.

"This will be hard to manage without shoes, but I'll do the driving," I tell Annabel as I stow the gun in the holster taped to my back and pat the seat. She pulls on the jacket and hikes up her skirt to mount the bike which is way too big for her. I place the helmet on her head and adjust the strap, then mount the bike in front of her.

"Hang on, sweetheart," I say and gun the engine, zooming in between cars.

About a half mile ahead, I see the police have blocked the exit and highway, and they're working their way back. I pull the motorcycle over to the far-left lane and stop it. "Get off."

Annabel dismounts. I follow, then heave the bike over the guardrail.

Annabel gasps. I pretty much gasp in my head, too—I shouldn't be able to lift a Harley Davidson in the air like that. Certainly not without straining something. But every day, it seems like my strength increases, along with endurance and heightened senses.

If I stay in the secret agent business, being a wolf could really come in handy.

But that's a huge *if*.

Annabel and I leap over the guardrail and climb back on.

The police catch sight of us and shout. I gun the motor-cycle, skidding out as we roar off in the opposite direction.

They'll have to do a lot better than a roadblock to catch me.

9

I CRANE my head to watch the lights of the cop cars recede behind us. Charlie drives like a madman, guiding the bike down narrow trashcan-lined alleyways. We don't stop until we're on a street lined with respectable brick townhouses.

"Think we lost them?"

Charlie shrugs. The wariness hasn't left his shoulders. With everything that's happened, I'm running out of shock, but the sight of him lifting the bike like it was a toy is forever burned into my brain.

I guess these super spies eat their Wheaties.

"Why are the cops looking for us?"

"Someone put a bulletin out. I'm burned, you're probably wanted as an accomplice."

I let my head sag against his shoulder. He reaches back and squeezes my knee.

"Let's get to the safehouse. Then we can work on clearing you and your father's name."

And figure out who sent men to grab me. I can't even deal with the thought of the wolf. I've reached my quota of crazy.

Charlie doesn't think I'm crazy. I'm actually surprised he didn't question me further about the wolf. Maybe he knows something I don't, and there's a new trend of using K9 units for surveillance and/or hit squads. What the hell else could it be?

By the time we reach the park where we're to meet Otis, my stomach has settled. I may not know what the hell happened back at the hotel, but one thing is clear—I feel perfectly safe with Charlie. Even when he whips the motorcycle through the tiniest possible spaces between traffic-stuck cars. Any other guy, I'd be screaming to get down, but with Charlie, I tuck my arms tighter around him, close my eyes and relax into the ride.

As the roar of the bike fills my ears, I tilt my face into the rushing wind. Charlie's hard abs flex against my forearms as he wheels and swerves the bike like a stunt devil. When we stop, my heart is pounding, and I feel a little weak, but not with fear. Charlie puts his legs down, steadying the bike for me to hop off, and I linger, bowing my head to catch a little of his man-and-leather scent.

Across the small park, Otis sits on a bench, eating peanuts. Reluctantly, I slide my arms from around Charlie's middle. He catches my hand and squeezes it, keeping it even as we stroll from the motorcycle. I'm still barefoot, but the grass feels nice.

"Nice bike," Otis drawls as we approach.

"Thanks, man." Charlie hooks his arm around my shoulders. "A friend let me borrow it—I promised to give it right back. You ever ride one?"

"Missus won't let me. Got a boring beige sedan." Otis hooks a thumb over his shoulder at the car parked under a row of maples, then holds up the brown bag. "Peanut?"

"Don't mind if I do." Charlie takes the bag. There's a slight clink inside. He offers it to me, and I slip my hand in, feeling the car keys inside there along with the peanuts. I grab the keys and nod to Charlie, who pulls the bag away, slipping the motorcycle key inside before handing the bag back to Otis. At least, I think he slips in the motorcycle key. I don't actually see anything even though I'm watching for it. We crack peanuts and eat them for a few seconds before Otis stands.

"Keep the rest." Otis dusts off his hands. No sign of the key although I'm sure he has it. These spy guys are better than street magicians. "I have to get home before the missus gets antsy. Wish I could be off to my fishin' shack. I always keep an overnight bag and map in the car, just in case I need to get away." He grins and ambles off.

"He'll do a few loops, watching to see if we've been followed," Charlie tells me.

"We'll take his car, right? And it'll have an overnight bag and map to his fishing shack?"

"Yep." With his hand on my elbow, Charlie steers me up the sidewalk toward the 'boring beige sedan' Otis pointed out. "We'll stop to get some clothes."

DUSK SETTLES by the time the car rolls down a long, dusty dirt road. The wheel hits a pothole, and I blink awake.

"Almost home," Charlie murmurs, and I flash him a little grin. I'm wearing a "Virginia is for Lovers" shirt, courtesy of a tourist shop. I wriggle my toes in my new, sparkly flip-flops. Out of D.C. traffic, on a nice back road near the Maryland coastline, I feel like I'm on vacation.

"If it wasn't for all the shooting and dead people, this spy stuff would be kinda fun," I tell him.

He nods, the corners of his mouth turning up. I sense he's been worried about my state of mind after the near-kidnapping, but once the adrenaline left my body, I dozed all the way from D.C. The little nap did me wonders.

It's crazy how much I trust Charlie. I couldn't have slept so easily next to anyone else in the world. I feel a little guilty, having the weight of my problems rest on his super spy shoulders, but he'll take care of them—I know it to my bones.

The car lights hit a small structure made of grey boards, leaning a little to the side.

"This is it," he announces after checking the map.

When I get out, I smell the salty, somewhat swampy scent of water. We're not quite on the ocean, just an inlet.

Otis gave us more than just a map to his place. Charlie pulls out burner phones, two laptops, and four guns. We have been resupplied.

"I need to check in with my sister. And call Flack," I realize. "He's probably wondering why I was a no-show."

"Set up another meeting for tomorrow," Charlie instructs. "We need to find out what he knows about American Trade Assets."

Charlie

I PICKED up steaks at the grocery on the way in, and light the grill. I bought four, but I swear, I could eat ten. Annabel's going to be on to me when she sees me wolfing—heh—these down.

Hell, I can't believe she hasn't put two and two together already. I guess werewolf is just so far out of people's minds as a real possibility, they refuse to see what is.

I'm speaking from experience, of course.

I was so sure my father and Nash had been the subject of some government gene modification or enhancement project. I just never put the wolf thing together. Not even with the memory of my father's death.

Not until I saw it with my own eyes.

I throw the steaks on the grill, along with corn on the cob still in the husk. Annabel comes out and hands me a beer.

"I didn't get Flack. Just left a message. Sarah and Grady are fine, just restless."

I clink the mouth of my beer bottle to hers. "Cheers."

She smiles, her expression soft and full of gratitude. "Charlie? Why are you doing this for me?"

"I owed you one." I deflect in an effort to ignore the discomfort of my heart squeezing in my chest.

She shakes her head. "You didn't owe me this much."

I stare through the trees at the water beyond. "You mean something to me," I say at last. My heightened senses note her held breath, her racing pulse. I turn to face her. "It's true. You have a life. Maybe you don't get out much, but you still have a family. A sister and a nephew. I have nobody—by design."

Her eyebrows draw together in concern, but she says nothing, lets me talk.

It comes as a relief, really, to unload my burden on her.

"My mom thinks I'm dead. As far as she knows, I died

serving my country ten years ago. I don't exist anymore. I can't maintain ties—you know that. So, in a twisted, pathetic way, you've become family to me." I open the grill and flip the steaks and corn.

Her lips part.

"That sounds creepy and stalkerish, doesn't it?" I laugh into my beer. "I'm not as mal-adjusted as it sounds, I promise. It's just that you're the only person I see on a regular basis. The only person who knows what I do. Where I am. How I live. When I asked you for help, you gave it. Without demanding answers."

"I demanded a favor in return." She sounds rueful.

"I was thrilled. I *wanted* to give something back to you. I guess I secretly craved more of a connection with another human being."

She nods, looking away, and I realize I said that wrong.

"No, not just any human being. With you. My beautiful, brilliant handler. The woman who gives me my orders and rides my ass when I miss a meetup."

"We don't even know each other," she says, but she's staring up at me with stars in her eyes. Like she's willing me to make her believe what I'm saying.

"I want to know more," I say honestly. "I want to know everything."

She looks away again, out to the water. "I always knew I'd fall for an agent." She sounds rueful like it's a bad thing. Which, I guess, it is.

It would be hard enough if I was just a spy, but considering my wolf problem, it's downright dangerous.

"I'm sorry." And I am. I never meant to pull her heart into play. Hell, I didn't even realize mine was in the game until it was far too late. I think I forgot I even had a heart, to be honest.

She shakes her head. "No, I am. I don't mean to be a downer. It just figures the only guy I'm ever attracted to is unavailable."

I frown. What is she talking about? "Why does that figure?"

She takes a long swing of beer. "I mean girls usually pick men like their daddies, right?"

"I see." I want to tell her I'll be different, to promise to be available, but of course, I can't. I have nothing to offer Annabel Gray. Not even my heart which wasn't much worth having, to begin with. No, I left my heart back in Kentucky the day I enlisted and became one of the government's human weapons.

Except it turns out I'm not human. I guess the joke was on them, huh?

I pull the steaks and corn off the grill. "Are you hungry, sweetheart?"

"Starved," she says.

Good. Because my monster is dying to feed you.

Whatever the fuck that's about.

Annabel

CHARLIE WATCHES me eat like it's an erotic act. His gaze never leaves my lips as he shovels food past his own.

Three steaks.

I'm not kidding you. The guy ate three steaks. It's incredible. He must have the highest metabolism in the history of the universe. Well, how else would he be able to lift a Harley Davidson over a concrete divider?

Spending this time with him is like getting wrangled into a thriller. I'm holding my breath, squeezing my eyes closed, but still enjoying the ride. Loving watching the strong, brave, and handsome hero defeat the bad guys. At least I hope that's how this one ends.

Charlie certainly makes me believe everything will come out all right even though logic tells me differently. When I stop and think about how deep I'm into this thing—how meaningless my life may soon become... Well, I can't think that way. It's too morbid. Plus, Sarah and Grady's lives hang in the balance too. So, Charlie and I *have* to figure this out. We have to make sure they can walk away unharmed when it's all over.

And Charlie, too. I should be more concerned about the trouble I've gotten him into.

"What are you thinking?" He has another beer open, sipping from the bottle.

"I'm worried about your job."

"Sweetheart," Charlie scoffs, "that's one thing you don't ever have to worry about."

"Why?"

"I can take care of myself. No matter what happens. Let's just worry about you. Plan our end game. We need definite proof about what happened in El Salvador. Then what? You want to take those responsible down?"

I chew on my lip. Do I? This started as a mission to find the truth. Now, am I going after justice?

"If you don't, they're going to keep coming for you, baby. You knocked over the wasp's nest. They're already swarming and stinging. There's no half-assing the rest of this. Either you finish them, or they'll finish you."

I think of my father. The starch of his uniform against my skin when he'd pick me up and hold me on his hip. The medals he wore on his chest. The hero I believed him to be. *Still* believe him to be.

He'd want me to do the right thing. For Sarah and Grady. For our country.

I lift my chin. "Yes. I'm going to take them down."

Charlie smiles like he already knew what I was going to say.

"That's my girl. So, let's get busy."

10

C *harlie*

IT'S LATE. I pace up and down the length of the cabin as Annabel's fingers fly on the keys. She's hacking back into the CIA, searching for anything we can find on who's behind American Trade Assets, the political action group that appeared on Director Scape's bank deposits.

My thoughts, normally so ordered and neat, are a jumbled mess. I'm sweating, practically feverish as if the moonlight is stronger than the sun, and it's burning me through the thin curtain hung over the rustic cabin window.

I need Annabel so bad, I'm sick. Nausea quakes in my belly, my fingernails dig into my skin. Not even the desire to shift and run can tear me from her side even as it kills me to be close to her. The muscles in my arms and legs begin shaking. Okay. I need to get out of here.

"I'm going for a run."

Annabel's fingers stop moving, and she turns. Whatever she sees in my face makes her draw back. She stands up and catches my arm.

"Charlie." There's fear on her face.

She should be afraid. Afraid of what will happen if I stay.

"I'm sorry, baby. I'm restless. And staying here with you... it's making me crazy."

Hurt creases her face, so I glance down at my rock hard bulging cock—awareness blooms.

She swallows at the same time she palms my crotch, taking me by painful surprise.

I groan. "Baby, I can't."

"You look like you could use some help with that."

"I could—I mean—*oh*."

She already has my zipper down, cock out and fisted.

I almost come right then. My hand tangles in her hair, pulling her mouth to it even as words like, "No... I can't..." rasp from my lips.

Then it's all over. She takes my cock between those beautiful, full lips, and my eyes roll back in my head.

"Christ, Annabel. Don't. I mean, *do*. Please. Oh, fuck." I thrust my hips forward like a jackass, gagging her with my cock, but I can't hold back. There's no way to stop the monster now that he's been let out.

My vision changes, her scent grows stronger in my nostrils.

Annabel.

Only Annabel.

My lovely, lovely Annabel.

I must have her.

Must. Claim.

I'm way too rough. Grasping the back of her head, I hold

her captive and fuck her mouth, shoving deeper and with more force every time.

A salty scent brings me up—tears from gagging glisten on her lashes.

Unacceptable.

Somehow, I manage to pull out of her mouth, to stumble back. But she moves with me.

The crazy, beautiful female won't allow me to retreat. She stands and follows me, shoving me down onto the sofa.

"Yes, no," I pant. Heat prickles all over my skin as Annabel shimmies out of her jeans and panties and straddles my lap.

She leans over and bites my ear. "Do you have a condom?"

I can't even decipher her breathy words. All I know is a mad desire to claim her in every possible position, in every orifice. To make sure she knows she belongs to me.

But that's not right. I can't lay claim to her like she's a piece of property. That's the monster talking.

Annabel searches my pockets, and I finally realize what she's after. I produce the condom. She rips open the foil packet and rolls the rubber over my massively erect cock.

I catch her and pull her down to my lap, claiming her mouth with a possessive, dominating kiss. She tastes like honey and apples. Like perfection. My tongue sweeps between her lips as I thrust my sheathed cock into the notch of her legs. I fill one palm with her ass, and she squirms over my throbbing manhood. I spin our bodies around. Lips locked, she tumbles back on the couch, my hand protecting the back of her head. I yank her into position and line my cock up with the place it's dying to be.

All the while, I can't stop kissing her. I bite her lower lip, lick her tongue, devour her. And when I sink into her wet heat, fireworks go off behind my eyes.

And they keep going off. I scythe in and out of her, every thrust a life-changing indulgence, every kiss a new promise.

Mine, the monster roars.

Mine, only mine.

Mine forever.

And Charlie's in here somewhere still, knowing it's not right, but I can't stop the wolf. He gets what he wants, and he wants Annabel.

She has no chance in hell of not being claimed tonight.

Mine, mine, mine.

Oh God, she feels so good. It's like I was born for exactly this moment. To be united with her, both body and soul. There's a communion here—it's so much bigger than sex. It's galaxies and worlds and every tiny particle in the universe wanting us to be together.

I'm certain of it.

Nothing could break us apart.

I fuck her and fuck her and fuck her.

She tips back her head and screams, and I cover her mouth, drag my palm over her beautiful lips, drop my thumb between them.

She sucks it.

I get the other hand up her t-shirt, where it wanted to be all night and pinch and pull her nipples.

I'm going to fuck her all night. After this fucking, I'll lick her to orgasm. Then I'll tie her to the bed and torture every inch of her body with my tongue. I'll keep her up singing, keep her screaming until the damn moon sets.

But then something momentous happens. Like a car crash or a rebirth. My body feels like it's being torn apart and put back together at the same time.

The monster roars.

I come.

Annabel comes.

Happiness flows through me. Pure joy.

Then my tongue's coated with blood, and Annabel's scream pierces the night.

∿

Annabel

PAIN RIPS THROUGH ME—A burning, gauging pain.

He bit me.

I don't believe it, but Charlie flies back and lands onto his ass on the floor, blood dripping from oversized canines.

And his eyes.

Ice. Blue.

Just like the wolf in the stairwell. Like the wolf at the cabin.

Cold gooseflesh runs across my arms. No. It can't be.

Werewolves don't exist.

But there's no other explanation. Charlie is a freaking werewolf!

And he bit me—the man I would've sworn this morning would protect me from anything.

"Get back!" I shout even though he's already retreated. Hands shaking, I grab the Glock from my purse and cock it. Blood soaks my t-shirt around my right shoulder.

Flashes of what I've already seen run through my mind. Charlie's need to go out alone for night runs. The wolf tearing at the door of the cabin. The wolf appearing in the stairwell while Charlie went off comms. It all fits.

I would've sworn nothing ruffles Charlie Dune, but right now, horror fills his eyes. He doesn't look ready to attack. He seems afraid—of what he's done.

"Shoot me," he whispers.

My two hands shake as I aim the gun between his eyes. My breath comes fast and shaky.

"Do it," he says, louder.

I try to keep a tough face on, but I feel one side of it crumple. I'm not a warrior like my dad or Charlie. I couldn't shoot the wolf between the eyes when it tried to get to me at the cabin. There's no way I can do it now when he's in human form and afraid. But I know he's not afraid of me. He's afraid *for* me. And that's the reason I keep the gun pointed.

"How long?" I shout. "How long have you been a wolf?"

"A month, I guess," he mutters.

"You guess?" My voice rises in pitch. "What the fuck, Charlie?"

"I don't know—maybe all my life. My dad was one. But I only started changing a month ago. After Honduras. I would've told you if I could've figured out how to make it sound believable in any way."

"So, am I a werewolf now, too?" I can't keep the wobble out of my voice.

Charlie wipes the blood from his lips. Remorse shows on every line of his face. "I don't know." His words are barely audible. "But you should put me down. Before I do it again."

I swallow. "I already shot you once," I rasp. "At the cabin."

He points to the center of his forehead. "Put it here, Annabel."

I should. Charlie Dune is out of control. He hurt me. He could hurt someone else. But killing isn't in my wheelhouse.

"Do it!" he roars.

I jerk when he shouts, but I still can't fire. A tear rolls down my cheek.

"Annabel, I'm a danger to you. I don't know what else I might do. You need to shoot me. I'd rather you did it than someone else. Please."

My finger tightens on the trigger.

But pulling it is an impossibility. Even when he's yelling at me to do it.

My lips tremble. "Get up." I gesture with the gun.

"Shoot me," he whispers again.

"Get up!" I put some authority in my command.

Charlie scrambles to his feet and cleans up—taking off the condom, tucking his cock away in his jeans.

"Get out." I point to the door with the gun.

"Annabel, I'll just come back. I'll find a way in. You're like a drug to me." He's pleading with me. He wants me to put him down.

I *can't.*

"Get. *Out.*"

Charlie walks to the door, opens it and steps through. "Lock this door, sweetheart," he mutters as he shuts it tight.

∾

Charlie

OH LORD, what have I done to Annabel? I wish to God she would've shot me.

I don't experience fear. I learned to shunt that into power long, long ago. But I'm more afraid for Annabel than I've ever been.

I hurt her.

I hurt my beloved.

Annabel.

My mind replays what just happened. How deep the wounds were where they were located. How much blood left her.

No, the wounds aren't fatal. If they don't get infected, she'll heal up, even without immediate medical intervention.

I stand on the porch and stare up at the moon.

What have I done?

The strange thing is, I have no urge to shift and run anymore. I'm calmer than I've been any night this week. More focused.

I climb into the truck we stole to get here. I'll spend the night here, watching over her. In the morning, I'll make myself invisible and follow her out, wherever she goes. I can't leave her unprotected. Not until this mission is over.

But I also can't put myself in the same room with her, either.

I'm a terrible danger to her.

Annabel

THE SHOCK of betrayal guts me even though I'm starting to believe Charlie couldn't control himself. I don't think he meant to hurt me.

I run for the bathroom and pull off my t-shirt to inspect the wounds. There are four puncture wounds, a half-inch deep.

Could've been worse. No major arteries. Not too much blood loss. I definitely feel woozy though.

I turn and heave into the toilet. The room spins. Oh God. Am I turning into a werewolf?

Will I start biting people at the full moon, too?

I stagger to the bedroom and fall down on the bed. My eyelids are heavy—too heavy to keep open. It's like I've had a few too many drinks and I'm passing out still liquored up.

Yep, passing out...

I WAKE TO A CREAKING FLOORBOARD.

Charlie?

Did he come back in? Of course, I locked the door, but Charlie Dune could get past any lock if he wanted to. I didn't think he would though.

And yet, relief is not a strong enough word for how I feel at the idea he's come back. It's more like celebration. Like everything was off in the world, and now it's right again.

The doorknob to the bedroom turns slowly, and the hair stands up on my head.

It's not Charlie.

My instincts take over, and I throw myself over the side of the bed, rolling under it just as the door creaks and swings wide.

Someone grunts and a body thuds to the floor.

Somehow, I stifle my scream.

The cabin shakes with gunfire in the living room. I crawl on my belly to retrieve the pistol on the night table. Based on the thuds and smacks of hand to hand combat, interspersed with gunfire from the front room, I think Charlie's here, silently fighting to protect me.

I try to turn on the lamp by the bed, but nothing happens—the electricity has been cut. I get up and run for the door, just as the glass shatters in the bedroom window, exploding with gunfire.

"Annabel?" Charlie shouts as I drop to the floor.

"One assailant, firing from outside." I'm amazed at how calm my report sounds.

Guns fire from the living room, and suddenly, Charlie's in the doorway, lit by a swath of moonlight from the window. "Stay low. Get behind the bed." I hear his soft footfalls and the crunch of glass as he runs to the wall beside the window and dodges out, gun leading. He fires twice, then drops the gun.

"Here." I slide mine across the floor to him, assuming he's out of bullets.

"Thanks." He picks it up and fires three more times. "There's at least two still out there. Three down."

I crawl toward the closet, remembering the duffel bag of weapons. When I open the door, Charlie joins me. "You take the semi-automatic. Give me two more pistols."

I yank them out with the magazines.

"Stay behind me." He moves through the cabin stealthily, and I follow behind, holding the weapon in both hands.

Gunshots ring out the moment he kicks open the door. He yanks me up against the wall between the door and window. I count the gunshots. Eight. Ten. Fourteen. Fifteen.

"Stay here." Charlie breaks through the door, a pistol in each hand, arms extended out straight in two directions. He fires four bullets.

One body drops.

"Cover me." Charlie disappears, running toward the dirt driveway where he parked the car we stole.

I don't really know how to do that, but I fire a round

toward the trees in the direction away from where Charlie ran. God forbid I accidentally hit him.

Except wait—bullets apparently can't harm him unless they're between the eyes.

I hear fists smacking flesh, grunts, and strikes. I creep out of the cabin in their direction, swinging the gun right and left defensively.

Behind the vehicle, Charlie's fighting with Director Scape.

"Don't move," I shout.

Both men ignore me. Charlie slams Scape up against a tree trunk and smacks his head against the wood.

"I kept you alive for this," Charlie says and punches Scape in the gut.

"Oof." He doubles over. "For what?"

"For Annabel. So, you can tell her the truth. Go on." He pounds a right hook into Scape's jaw.

Director Scape spits blood from his mouth and laughs. "The truth? The truth is whatever I want it to be. I run the fucking CIA."

"Who killed my father?" I demand. It's not the question I thought I would ask, but it's the one that comes out.

Scape laughs. "I did. I killed your father when he disobeyed orders."

I shouldn't be holding this weapon. Because I am way too ready to use it. "What orders?" I grit between clenched teeth.

Charlie punches Scape again.

"He had orders to destroy the village. Restart the war. He didn't comply. I had to go in and clean it up for him."

"Who gave those orders? You?"

Scape gives another bloody smile. His hand flashes out before I realize I've stepped too close. He swings the butt of my weapon around to point at Charlie and squeezes the trigger.

Charlie grasps Scape's head and breaks his neck, even as blood spurts out his shoulder and side.

"Charlie!" I scream.

"I'm okay. I'm fine." He covers the wound in his side with his hand while he toes Scape's limp body as if to make sure he's really dead.

Apparently unconcerned with his bullet wounds, Charlie pulls his phone from his back pocket and hands it to me. The recorder is on—he got the whole confession.

"We've got it. You're free now."

Charlie

I TAKE Scape's phone and wallet and pocket them. I already searched the men inside the cabin. None of them carried IDs or phones. I need to find their vehicle.

I sniff the air. I'm getting better at identifying the different scents around me, and I don't detect any new humans. I've dealt with them all.

I check the body of the guy I shot in the trees. He's dead, no ID.

"Let's get you inside," I say carefully. Annabel hasn't moved, and I scent her fear and shock. I don't know if she will even let me in that cabin with her, but I have to at least make sure she's unharmed. The urge to care for her is overwhelming. Once I know she's safe, that she can safely return to her life and her family, I will leave. I need to get away from anyone I could hurt.

"Are-are they all dead?"

I smell only death. I nod. Even though the danger is over, my body is still tense. I'm wary of any further danger to my mate.

Mate? That's a strange word choice.

I find their vehicle a hundred yards up the dirt road. It has the IDs and phones of the other men. I take them all. When I get back to the cabin, I flip the breaker in the electrical box. The lamp in the bedroom flares to life.

Annabel still hasn't moved like she's afraid to go in alone.

I walk to her, reaching out cautiously. She tumbles forward into my arms.

"Charlie," she chokes.

"It's okay." I stroke her silky hair. "It's over now. Everything is over."

The scent of her blood from the wounds I inflicted stings my nose, making my chest collapse in on itself.

She sniffs, her tears wet against my neck. "Now what?"

I straighten, pulling away to wipe her tears. "Now you go in. Turn yourself into someone you trust. Make copies of that recording, so there's no getting rid of you. You'll be safe. Your sister and nephew can go home. You can go back to your job."

Her lips tremble. "What about you?"

Damn.

I'd rather cut off my arm than leave Annabel. But I'm not safe for her.

"I'll disappear."

Pain creases her forehead. "What does that mean?"

"I need to get this wolf thing figured out. Before anyone else gets hurt." My eyes fall on her blood-soaked shirt, and her fingers reach to lightly touch the bite marks.

"Are there others you can talk to? Find out how to get rid of it? Or what to do to eliminate the effects?"

I think of Jared and the wolf pack in Tucson. "Maybe." I nod. "Yes. that's where I'll go first."

"Where are they?"

I touch her nose. "I'm not telling you that, angel. Disappear means disappear."

Her jaw firms and she lifts her chin. "I might be able to help. I'd like to help."

I'm not sure how I keep standing. The earth seems to shake and crumble beneath my feet. I cup her nape and lean my forehead against hers.

"I'll be sure to ask if I need anything," I promise, but it's a lie.

We both know this is goodbye.

Forever.

"What if I need you?" Her voice rises. "What if I turn into a wolf and start attacking people, too?"

"You know how to get a message to me." All clandestine agents have servers we check for messages. I can keep checking mine even if I stay rogue. "I'll message you with anything I find out that's pertinent to your bite. I promise."

"So, this is it?" Her voice chokes, and I nearly drop to my knees.

I stroke her cheek with my thumb. "I love you, Annabel Gray."

It seems important to tell her. Especially since I'll never see her again. She should know the truth.

"Charlie," she chokes.

"It's okay. You don't have to say anything. I just wanted you to know. This wasn't some mission hook up for me. It was about as far from that as it gets."

Tears spill from Annabel's beautiful gray eyes. "Me too."

I cup her face with both hands and thumb away the tears.

"You need me, I'll come. That's a goddamn promise."

"I know," she chokes.

My eyes sting. "Good." I pray to God she never needs me though.

No, that's a lie, but I can't even hope for another shot with Annabel. That fantasy will absolutely kill me.

I move in slowly, my lips hovering above hers. "Goodbye, Annabel."

She darts in for a quick peck, then pulls away, turning her back on me. "Goodbye."

nnabel

I DRIVE out of the woods with my heart on the floor mat. Letting Charlie walk off into the sunrise nearly killed me. I wanted to run after him, offer to drive him someplace, give him a warm meal. But I know he needs none of those things. If there's any guy who can survive on his wits alone, it's Charlie Dune.

It's probably stupid that I'm clinging to hope he'll find some solution to his wolf problem and show back up in my life. Even without the wolf thing, the idea would be ludicrous. It's not who he is. He's a work-alone spy. A deadly government weapon.

He was never going to move in with me and start up a sweet little relationship. He was never going to stick around.

And I knew that from the get-go.

So, why then do I feel like I just jumped off a cliff and am lying flat on the desert floor below?

I grab a burner phone and call Sarah.

"Annabel!" she cries. "Please tell me we can leave this godforsaken cabin."

"Yep. You're free."

"Hallelujah! Grady and I are going nuts here. Not that I wasn't totally freaked out about your safety. Except I was only a little freaked out because I knew you had your super agent with you. How is that hunk of man-chest, anyway?"

"Um, okay." My voice wavers.

"Oh shit, Bel, what happened?"

"Nothing. He just had to go."

"Asshole."

"No, it's not like that. Really. Not at all." I touch the wounds on my shoulder. "He just has his own personal demons he has to deal with."

Then I'm crying like a freaking baby.

"Oh Bel, I'm so sorry. He seemed like a great guy. And really into you."

I swipe at my tears. "Yeah. Definitely a great guy. Exactly what I'd want in a partner. Too bad I always want the kind of guys who can't be partners."

"Like Dad," Sarah says softly. She picked a military man for a husband, too. And she lost him to the military. He never wanted to come home and be a dad.

"Yeah, I guess you know all about that, too."

We're silent together, just acknowledging each other's pain. Our own pain.

"Well, I found out who really killed dad."

Sarah draws in a sharp breath. "Tell me."

I tell her the entire story, leaving nothing out which takes me the length of the drive back to Washington, D.C.

"So, what are you going to do now?"

"I think I'm going to call Senator Flack. Bring him the recording and see if he can tell me where to go from here. Right after I check into a hotel and have a really long cry."

"You want me to come out there? A real shoulder to cry on? Grady and I will be on a plane in a second."

I tear up again, my chest squeezing. "No, you and Grady need to get home. But thank you. I love you."

And like a crazy woman, I burst into tears again. "He said he loved me," I tell her. "And I didn't say it back."

Sarah makes a sympathetic sound. "I'm sure he knows. You're not so good at hiding your feelings."

"Yeah, but I wish I'd told him."

"Do you have any way to contact him?"

I sniff. "Yes. But I'd have to speak in code."

"Well, if it's important to you, get him the message. Let him know you'll be around if he gets his shit figured out. I mean, if that's what you want."

I don't *want* that to be what I want. Waiting around for how long? Months? Years? Never knowing if Charlie's dead or alive? It sounds terrible. And yet the alternative—crushing the hope, however dim it may be, of ever seeing him again—is far worse.

"Yeah, maybe. Thanks, Sarah."

"Call me again. Let me know when you have a phone number I can use again."

"I will. Love you, sis."

"Love you."

I park the stolen truck in a Sheraton parking lot and get out. Time for a shower. A long cry. And to go on.

Without Charlie in my life.

It seems impossible, but it's what I must do.

Charlie

I RIDE my new motorcycle to the metal warehouses south of the train tracks where the Tucson shifters set up their illegal cage fights. I'd made a new ID and taken the first flight I could get to Arizona where I bought this bike. I figure it will help me fit in, to connect with the pack.

The truth is, I like the way it feels—the power and speed remind me of what it's like to shift and run. Which must be why the shifters like them so well.

Several motorcycles are parked out front. I park beside them and dismount. I'm itchy about going in. Even in special forces, I was a lone wolf. It's not that I don't make friends, but I'm not a highly social guy.

Or maybe I hesitate because my heart's been smashed to a pulp, and I'm barely a shell of a man right now. But I need to go in there for Annabel, to find out what's going to happen to her—what's going to happen to me.

I push open the door without knocking, and four huge guys stop talking to look over.

I recognize them all from the last time I was here. I've been trained to never forget a face. Jared stands beside his pierced friend. Garrett Green is the pack leader, the one whose lawyer girlfriend marched in and pulled Jared out of the police station. The fourth guy is huge—built like a tank, complete with a military crew cut. He served as a bouncer at the cage fight.

"Well, well, well, he survived the full moon," Jared drawls.

His buddy snickers. "What'd you think? You were going to go on a killing rampage?"

I'm all out of humor. I march over and wrap my fist in the guy's shirt. He growls and the other three step forward, closing us in.

"I bit a girl. Could've killed her."

"You marked her," Jared speaks. His words cut through my anger. He's saying something important.

I release his friend's shirt and whirl. "I *what?*"

"You marked her as your mate. She survived it?"

I grip Jared's shirt. I'm ready to punch him for speaking so casually about Annabel almost dying.

"You should've fucking told me!"

Jared's big hand reaches for my throat, and it's on. I'm *dying* to grapple right now. I duck out of his reach and kick him in the gut. The other three move back, arms folded over chests.

"Did she survive?" he grits as he staggers back.

"Yeah, no thanks to you." I throw a punch. He dodges and swings at me. I drop down to sweep a foot out, tripping him to the ground. He's up in a blink, coming at me, both fists swinging. I duck and parry, try to get a swing into his ribs, but he blocks it.

"I tried to tell you. You hung up on me. I even called you back."

I remember now, the phone ringing as I crushed it beneath my heel.

Damn. I want this to be Jared's fault, but it's not. It's nobody's but mine.

I duck, but he goes in for my torso, picks me up and walks me backward to the wall, throws me against it.

I reach up to grab a beam, wrap my lower legs around Jared's neck and squeeze.

"So, what's going to happen to her?" I demand.

He grabs my legs and attempts to pry them off his throat.

"She's... forever marked... with your scent," he grits out with choked breath. "No... other wolf... will touch her."

I release him and drop to the ground.

"That's it? She's not going to turn into a wolf?"

All four wolves snicker. "We're not leeches, dude. You can't turn someone into a wolf," the pierced guy says.

"Unless you're the crazy Doctor Smyth," Garrett mutters.

Relief almost turns my legs weak. "So... she's fine? Other than the scent thing?"

Jared throws a right uppercut, and I let it land because I pretty much deserve it. It hits me on the left side of my jaw and throws me backward.

A good-natured grin spreads across his face. "You took that one on purpose, didn't you?"

I shrug.

He holds out a hand, and I take it. He pulls me forward.

"Guys, this is Agent Charlie Dune. I've told you about him." He introduces me to the other men. The pierced one is Trey, the larger one aptly called Tank.

"Well, you want the good news or the bad news?" Jared asks.

"Bad."

"Bad news is once you've marked a female, you'll never be able to leave her. She's yours to protect until you both die. The instinct will be there even if the human in you wants to deny the connection."

I blink. Could be worse. Could be way worse.

"But I won't hurt her? I won't bite her again?"

"You'll never hurt her. You'll kill to keep her safe," Tank says.

"I would anyway."

Garrett, Jared, and Tank all grin and nod like they know exactly how I feel.

"What's the good news?"

"Good news is now you won't go moon mad. The madness comes from denying the urge to mate—refusing your natural instinct. You've marked her—it's done. We won't have to babysit you over the next full moon."

I can hardly believe it. I'm not a danger—not to Annabel. Not to anyone.

The urge to rush back to Annabel's side is so strong, I have to work to keep myself in one spot.

Garrett's lips twitch. "What's her name?"

"Annabel. And, ah, I need to let her know all this. Right away. Thanks for the information, guys. I'll be in touch."

Trey snorts. "Next time stay for a beer."

"Yeah," I call over my shoulder as I start to leave. "I'd like that. Thanks."

"Dune," Garrett calls me back.

I turn. "Yeah?"

"Wolves need a pack. Especially a new wolf like you."

I frown. What the hell kind of fraternity thing is this? "Thanks, but I, ah, generally work alone."

"Yeah, I get that. But if you would've come to see us sooner, we could've helped with the moon madness. Or at least explained what was happening."

He's right. I was the asshole who refused to stop and ask for directions. I definitely screwed things up with Annabel because I was playing lone wolf.

"Are you saying you'd let me in your pack?"

Garrett shrugs. "You have a place here if you want. You helped get Nash's kid back. And it would be nice for us to have someone on the inside of the law for a change."

I shake my head. "I'm leaving the CIA. And I got a female to protect."

Female. Now I'm talking like them.

"Say," I'm not on the job anymore, but I can't stop asking. "You know anything about a Lucius Frangelico? Is he one of your—our kind?"

Garrett bares his teeth. "Hardly. He's a fucking leech."

I stare at him for a moment before I understand. "Oh, you've got to be kidding me. *Vampires* are a real thing, too?"

"Yeah, and this one is trouble," Trey says. "What do you know about him?"

I don't mind sharing information with these guys. I figure I owe them something for their help. "The CIA ordered a watch on him, but he made me every time I got close. I got pulled off the case, and I heard the next agent wound up dead."

Trey whistles.

"He's suspected of a number of things, including drug and weapons trafficking, but I don't think the government really knows what he's up to."

"He's opening a nightclub downtown in direct competition with the two other paranormal bars," Trey offers. "And he's made it clear he wants to be master of the city and hunt in our territory. We're not happy." His eyes glitter with a weird light as his monster peers out.

"No," Garrett growls, and the air vibrates with the same energy I feel right before I shift. "Not happy at all."

"Watch your backs. Let me know if I can help," I find myself offering.

Strange. Maybe this pack idea is growing on me.

"That'd be hard considering I don't have a working number for you," Jared says drily.

I pull out my phone and send him a message as I walk

backward toward the door. "There. Now you have it. I'll expect you to use it."

Jared's grin appears reluctant. "That almost sounds like you want to see us again."

I chuckle as I head out the door. "Yeah. Maybe I do."

Annabel

I DRAG through the motions of living. Check into the Sheraton. Get some new clothes. Shower. Feed myself.

It all feels like swimming through mud.

My mind is forever circling Charlie. Wishing I'd said I loved him. Wondering where he is. If he needs help. If he's a danger to others.

Did I do the right thing not putting him down?

I have to believe I did. His mind and rational thoughts were intact—he just struggled with animal urges. He'll figure it out.

Except guilt gnaws at me.

I should be with him, helping him figure it out.

The way he helped me.

Why did I let him go off alone? He needs me.

I force myself to move forward, the way I know Charlie expects me to. I make multiple copies of the confession to safeguard it, then log in and file an official CIA report on what went down with Director Scape, leaving out the parts about Charlie's wolf problem. I don't leave my contact information—not yet. I'm probably completely safe now, but I need to be sure.

I want to take it to the highest level possible to make sure this all comes out clean.

I call Senator Flack and leave a message.

He calls back right away.

"Annabel, my dear. Where are you?"

"I'm still in town, Senator. I have some information to share with you about my dad's death. Some new developments that involve the CIA. I wasn't sure where else to go, so I thought maybe you—"

"Of course, of course." He has that reassuring Santa Claus voice that puts me at ease. "I'm tied up in meetings today but why don't you come to my house later tonight, Annabel?"

"Sure, okay. That sounds great. What's the address?"

He gives it to me, and I end the call.

Now to send a message to Charlie.

Charlie

IN A MOTEL ROOM, I pull out my tablet to contact Annabel. I need to let her know she's safe and what this means. I don't know how she'll take the marking thing. If she wants me to stay away, I will. As long as I know she's safe, I'll respect her wishes.

I log into the secure server we have for messaging, enter my password, and provide a retinal scan.

She's already left me one. *I wish I'd said it—you know what I mean.* I smile. Then read, *I'm going to F with the recording tonight. He should have the authority to ensure everything comes out right before I return.*

A prickle of fear rolls over me. It's not attached to any rational thought—just a knowing. Something's not right. Is Annabel still in danger?

Oh, Lord. How could I have left her unprotected?

Fuck, fuck, fuck. I yank electronics out of my bag, plug in my phone, tablet, laptop. I get into the records from Director Scape's phone and from Agent Tentrite's and scan through them. There are calls from Scape to Tentrite. That's to be expected. I'm looking for anything from Flack. When did Annabel first call him?

I don't have Annabel's call records because she used a destroyed burner phone. I do have Scape's cell phone. And I have a good memory. I pinpoint the time Annabel would've called Flack, then check Scape's incoming calls.

There's one. Only a few seconds long. I download the recording and play it.

It's short and sweet. Simply the Senator's deep voice saying, "Call me on a secure line."

I grab Scape's cell phone and scroll through. Bingo, Director Scape made a call from his cell phone to that same number thirty seconds later.

Too bad I didn't have a bug on that phone.

But it's enough. Flack's involved. I have to get a message to Annabel before she goes there tonight.

I memorized the numbers on the burner phones Annabel and I bought, and I dial them all, one by one now. She doesn't pick up.

Dammit.

I leave a message on the server. *Do not go in to see F. Repeat, do NOT go in. Wait for further contact.* I leave a string of numbers in which my phone number is hidden in code. It could be broken by the CIA, but it might take them a little time.

Shoving my things back into a bag, I jump on the motorcycle and gun it for the airport. Flying East in the afternoon from Tucson is going to be a challenge, but hopefully, there's something going out. Why in the hell did I come all the way to Tucson instead of picking up the damn phone to call Jared, instead?

I'm an idiot.

~

Annabel

IT'S EIGHT P.M. when I get dropped off by my Lyft driver in front of the Senator's house. It's a showy, manicured estate in Georgetown. Much nicer than a former CIA director turned senator should be able to afford. He must come from money.

I clutch my attaché case and walk up the sidewalk. The door swings wide and the senator steps out with a warm smile.

"Annabel Gray. Come in, come in. You have your father's eyes."

"Do I?"

"Come in, have a seat." He gestures to an overstuffed sofa. "My wife is out tonight, but I can play host. Would you like something to drink?"

"No, nothing."

He sits down in the chair beside me and balances one ankle on his knee. "I'm glad we finally get to meet. Are you feeling better?"

"Yes. Actually, I lied when I said I had the stomach flu. Someone tried to stop me from seeing you."

His bushy white eyebrows raise above penetrating brown eyes. He leans forward.

"What happened?"

"Two guys pulled me into a stairwell. I got away but decided I'd better lie low until I put the pieces of this together."

"All right. Start from the beginning. Pieces of what? You mentioned your dad's death?"

"Yes. Senator Flack, you were director of the CIA when he died, right?"

"That's right."

"And do you know what his mission in El Salvador was?"

"He was quelling unrest, so the peace accord would go through."

"Actually, he was given orders to stir things up and prevent peace. And when he refused, his superior, Director Scape had him killed."

Flack sits back, a look of disbelief on his face. "That's quite an allegation."

"I have his recorded confession." I hold up my cell phone and hit play.

Flack's expression remains blank as he listens. Then he leans forward.

"Who have you told about this?"

It's an odd question. The wrong question. Isn't it? I'm suddenly ready to jump out of my skin with nerves. I lie to test him. "No one. I don't know who I can trust in the CIA. I came straight to you."

He clasps his hands. "That's good. And what about your partner? Where is he?"

My chest seizes. I can hardly breathe. He definitely shouldn't know anything about Charlie.

"What partner?"

"Oh, I assumed you had one of your field agents on this with you," he says smoothly. It's so smooth, I can't quite decide if I'm being paranoid or not.

"Nope. Totally alone." I clutch the edges of the attaché case in my lap. "I wouldn't involve agents on a personal matter. That would be unethical. Um, may I use your restroom?"

Senator Flack stands up. "Of course, right this way."

I follow his directions and shut myself in the bathroom. I just need a minute to think. To get my heart rate down, figure out what to do next. I stare at myself in the mirror, still surprised to see myself blonde.

Okay, I just need to leave. If there was a bathroom window, I'd already be out it. I wish I had a phone number for Charlie. But he's already out of town. I have to figure this one out on my own.

And I can. All it takes is staying calm. If I keep my wits about me, I can figure out for sure if the Senator is a part of things. I take a page out of Charlie's book and turn the recorder on my phone.

Here goes nothing.

I step out of the bathroom and pain explodes at the back of my head.

The last thing I remember is the floor rushing up to meet my face, then I'm out.

Charlie

I SEE the four meatheads hustling out of the Grand Cherokee parked in front of Senator Flack's house, weapons in clear view. They're private mercenaries by the look. Military trained. Probably from a high-profile, top-secret security company.

Hopefully, their presence means Annabel's still alive. I race around the side of the manor, climbing up to look in each window.

Oh God.

Annabel's on the living room floor, her wrists, ankles, and mouth taped with duct tape. The four goons stand around her, jawing with Senator Flack. I'm going to kill them all.

There are bars on the windows or I'd bust through this one right now.

I need a distraction. I grab a grenade from the duffel Otis packed for me, light it, and throw it into the front yard, then race to the back of the house. The grenade explodes, and the men inside the house shout and run out the front door. It takes me thirty-five seconds to pick the lock on the back door.

My wolf hearing detects someone on the other side of the door, so I throw it hard and smack him with it. The guy stumbles back. I kick his gun out of his hand and punch him in the face. He lunges for the gun on the floor, and I slam my boot into his back, flattening him with inhuman strength. He's out cold. Picking up the gun, I tuck it in the back waistband of my pants and race forward on stealthy feet. Three shots and the other guys are down. Their shots go wild. Senator Flack fires on me from behind the couch, but I dart behind the door frame.

Annabel stirs on the floor, and her eyelids flutter open. Thank fuck. I heard her heartbeat but seeing her lifeless made my wolf insane.

I need to eliminate Flack's threat to her.

I dive into the living room, rolling in front of her body and crouching, gun pointed. I take a bullet to the chest and return fire. Call me old school—I always aim straight between the eyes.

Flack drops to the ground.

I use shifter strength to tear off the duct tape around Annabel's wrists and ankles and wince with her when I pull it off her mouth. She throws herself at me, and I gather her in my arms, crushing her body against mine.

Sirens sound outside.

"Annabel. Christ. I almost lost you," I choke. "I never should have left you unprotected."

"You saved me," she breathes. "I knew you would. I mean, it wasn't rational—I didn't *think* you could possibly come to my rescue, but I knew. When I heard the explosion outside, something in me said, *See? He's here.*"

"Get on the floor, face down!" The police charge in, guns drawn.

nnabel

I DON'T WALK out of FBI custody until noon the next day. It took some red tape to cut through, but with the recording on my phone of Senator Flack ordering his lackeys to kill me, and my boss, Agent Tentrite presenting the report I filed yesterday, they released me without charge.

Tentrite escorts me out, a comforting hand on my shoulder. "I'm sorry about wiping that file on your dad and telling you to back off. I should've questioned my orders a little closer."

"No, I understand. You were just doing your job." I look around the busy lobby. "Where's Agent Dune?" I ask. "Has he been released?"

"Yes, he walked an hour ago. He turned in his resignation."

My heart plummets. He'll be leaving again. He has to.

Just because he came back to save me doesn't mean he can stay.

And yet the idea of letting him go again is like my face scraping concrete.

I walk outside and blink in the sunlight, fumbling with my phone to call a Lyft. My ride is accepted immediately, and it tells me the driver, Tom is one minute away. I watch for the white Honda Accord, a heavy pit in my stomach.

Charlie didn't even wait for me. Did he leave a message? I fumble with my phone, trying to get onto our private server. The white car pulls up. I step toward it without looking up from my screen.

A deep, familiar voice says, "Where to, ma'am?"

My head flies up. "Charlie!" I throw myself at him with a strangling hold.

His teasing grin dissolves into something more serious. "Annabel." He cups the back of my head, and I wince when he touches the bruise left by Senator Flack.

"You're hurt." Fury blazes in his eyes.

"Flack knocked me out." I rub the place. "I don't know what he hit me with."

"You should've been taken to the hospital for a once-over, not kept here overnight."

I smile at his vehemence. "Thanks, but I'll be okay." I look at the running car. "So, what? You already have a new job?"

His lips twitch. "I may have borrowed a Lyft driver's car for a few hours. I wanted to be the one to pick you up."

"How'd you know I ordered a Lyft?"

He shrugs. "I have my ways."

"I was afraid you left," I admit, dropping my eyes when my voice wobbles.

He lifts my chin. "Did you... want me to stick around?"

It's the first time I've seen Charlie Dune look vulnerable, and it attacks my heart in a way I didn't know was possible. It lends me strength—courage. I grab his shirt in both my fists and twist.

"I'm not letting you go figure your wolf thing out on your own. I'm going with you. Wherever you go. I know you like to work alone, but that's tough. You might need me. Even if it's to... put you down." It's a lie. I could never shoot Charlie, but I'm feeding him what I think he might accept from me.

To my surprise, he grins. "Is that so?"

I haven't seen him this jaunty since he showed up and ate my ice cream cone. It's a look I happen to adore on him.

I stand on my tiptoes and lean my face up to his. "Yes."

"What about your job?"

"I'll turn in my resignation, too."

He claims my lips in that passionate way of his—a firm, demanding kiss. "That's good, baby. Because I found out something about that bite I gave you."

I stiffen. Oh God, I'm going to be a wolf, too. Well, as long as I'm with Charlie, I'm up for anything.

"What did you find out?"

His gaze is tender. He strokes my cheek with his thumb.

"It means you're mine. Forever. I marked you with my scent so no other wolves will touch you."

Laughter bubbles up from my lips. "What? That's ridiculous."

He shrugs, smiling. "Ridiculous but true. And the reason I was going crazy, scratching to get in the cabin that night is my wolf had already chosen you as my life mate. He needed to seal the deal or else he'd go moon mad."

I roll my eyes, laughing. "And I'm not given a choice in the matter."

Charlie sobers. "Of course, you are. If you tell me to go

away, I'll..." He rubs his forehead. "Well, actually, I'm not sure I can leave you now, angel. But I would do my best if you insisted."

I've never felt so light in my life. The man I thought would never settle down, could never be pinned to one place or person is telling me he'll never leave. It's more than I ever hoped for. I choke up.

"Charlie..."

He studies my face, his body language changing slightly, drawing back. "It's okay. I won't hold you to anything. I promise."

"No." I shake my head. "I have to bear these scars." I touch my shoulder where he bit me. "You damn well better stick around."

"Yeah?" I've never seen such a wide grin on his face. It's spectacular.

"Yeah. I've always wanted my very own secret agent man. Now I have one."

"At your service," he murmurs, looping one arm around my waist and drawing my body right up against his.

"Did you really quit?"

He nods. "Yeah. It would be hard to keep watch over you if they were constantly sending me all over the globe on missions.

"What will you do for work?"

He shrugs. "I have plenty of money. We don't have to work unless you want to."

I blink up at him in surprise. "H-how?"

"Secret agent salaries can be pretty flexible, considering the job and risk involved. And my living expenses have been paid for since the day I enlisted. All my money has been in offshore accounts, growing interest. We're rich."

He said *we.*

There's a *we.*

I can hardly believe it. "We are?"

"Rich enough. Where do you want to live, angel?"

"I don't care," I answer without thought. "As long as I'm with you."

EPILOGUE

C harlie

ANNABEL and I slide in behind Sarah and Grady on the Space Mountain ride. Taking them to Disneyland was the first thing Annabel wanted to do when we left D.C. I guess she's been promising a family trip for years.

I'm loving it. Every slice of apple pie Americana I get feels like I've won the lottery. It's the life I never thought I'd have—the cotton candy, the girl, the kid. Well, he's not ours, but a nephew is close enough.

And I'm all about getting to know Annabel's family. I want to absorb everything that is Annabel for the rest of my life.

After this, we're going to Kentucky to visit my mom. Hopefully, she won't have a heart attack when she finds out I'm still alive. I want to hear from her the story about my dad —everything she knows. And I want to make up for the years I stole from her. Well, I probably can't ever do that, but I'm going to try my best.

The ride starts up, the roller coaster sliding over the tracks. "You're not going to scream like a girl, are you?" Annabel asks me. She's dyed her hair back to the dark auburn I love so much. I burrow my fingers into it and massage the back of her head.

"Oh, assuredly." I grin like an idiot.

"I am, too," Sarah says, putting her arms in the air and pasting on the terrified/excited face she'll be wearing for real in a few seconds.

The cars streak off into the darkness, and I turn Annabel's face toward mine, capturing a bumpy, breathless kiss.

"This is what it's always like with you," she shouts over the rattle of the tracks and the screams of the passengers.

"What?" I shout back.

"A rollercoaster ride I don't want to end."

I capture her face with both hands and find her mouth again, holding my lips against hers while we ride over the bumps and turns.

Same here, sweetheart.

Same here.

Epilogue II

Annabel

THIS IS the most tense I've seen Charlie. I find it fascinating and somewhat swoon-worthy that the guy doesn't flinch in life or death situations, it's the emotional ones that get him.

And yeah, showing up to tell your mom you're not actually dead must be a doozy.

We drive to a beautiful but rustic cabin-style mountain home and get out of the SUV we rented in Lexington.

"Wow, is this the house you grew up in?" I ask before I realize it's probably too new for that.

Charlie doesn't take his eyes off the structure as he shakes his head. "They arranged a big pension payout for her when I died. It was part of our negotiations."

Oh God—he died. This woman grieved her only son. What will she think when we just show up at her door?

The door opens, and a slender woman in her early fifties comes out, suspicion crawling over her expression.

We walk toward the house, but every step seems to take forever.

"Forgive me, mama," Charlie says, but he doesn't speak loud enough for her to hear.

She's looking at me with narrowed eyes, her hands on her hips. Her gaze swivels to Charlie, and she freezes.

He nods, still walking glacially slow. "It's me, mama. I'm alive."

Her gaze jerks back to me, then she's in motion, flying down the steps and throwing herself at Charlie. He wraps his arms around her and squeezes, his eyes moist.

"Charlie? How can this be? You're really alive? What's going on?"

"I'm sorry, mama," he murmurs again.

She pulls back sharply to look at his face. Hers is streaked with tears. "You're sorry for what? What the hell is going on?"

"I went into the CIA. Clandestine services. They killed me off for your protection. I'm so sorry."

She opens and closes her mouth twice before she turns to me and says, "Well, I guess you both had better come in."

She leads the way, and I squeeze Charlie's hand. I can tell this is unbelievably painful for him because he's practically turned to stone. His movements are mechanical and stiff, his face blank, his eyes vacant.

She ushers us into a beautiful, high-ceilinged log cabin and brings out three bottles of beer. "I guess it's early to be drinking, but..." she trails off, staring at her son.

He opens his beer and chugs half of it.

"I'm Annabel," I say, sticking out my hand.

She jerks her gaze back to me and gives my hand a warm squeeze. "I'm Callie. Are you Charlie's girl?"

"Yes, I am." My hand subconsciously slips to my shoulder where the bite marks have become subtle scars, and her eyes track the movement. Her expression sharpens and turns on her son.

"Charlie, are you—" she breaks off, uncertainty flashing on her expression.

"A wolf?"

Her lips part, eyes grow wider.

"Yes."

She throws her arms back around his neck, and he closes his eyes when he holds her, as if in pain.

"I should have told you, Charlie. I just didn't think you'd become one. I didn't know."

"I should've told you I was alive. I'm sorry for the pain I caused you."

She leans against him as if her legs won't work. Tears flow freely down her face. "Don't you be sorry, boy," she says fiercely. "You're alive. That's all that matters to me now."

He kisses the top of her head, the stiffness ebbing from his shoulders and face. "You forgive me?"

She takes his hand and leads him to the couch, waving me to sit down, too. "There's nothing to forgive. You served your country. I couldn't be more proud. But what changed? Why are you here now?"

"I quit. It may still be unwise for me to be here, but I couldn't stay away."

She sits beside him and squeezes his hand. "I'll bet you have some questions about your father, too."

"I do. Tell me, mama."

"I met him in the woods outside your grandfather's place. I was sixteen. This giant silver wolf was tracking me.

"It scared the hell out of me. I ran, and he gave chase. I don't think he could help himself—he had raging teen hormones, and the moon was full.

"He disappeared when I got to the house. I locked the door and told your grandparents, but they didn't believe me. No one did. Wolves aren't supposed to live in these mountains.

"I didn't see him again for two years, then he came into the bar as a man and asked me out. We dated for a couple months. Things got intimate. Then one full moon, he bit me." She pulls back the collar of her shirt to show marks just like mine.

"I freaked out. Got out of his truck and ran home, bleeding. He tried to follow to explain, but your grandpa went after him with a shotgun.

"I didn't see him again until after you were born. I had my own place, and I saw the wolf again. I went and got a gun, and he changed—right there, in front of my eyes. The wolf became a man.

"He tried to explain to me what had happened—that

wolves mark their mates, except he shouldn't have marked me because I was a human. He said it was forbidden to mark a human, and his family was furious he'd fathered a child.

"He wanted to see you. I told him no way. I was afraid, Charlie. I thought his kind would come and try to take you away from me. I did my best to keep him out of your life.

"But he cared about you." Her eyes—the same cash green as Charlie's—fill with fresh tears. "He never stopped trying to see you. To convince me he wasn't bad. Then—" she stops speaking her voice choking.

"Then he got shot by Grandpa," Charlie finishes flatly.

I gasp.

Callie nods. "You saw it, didn't you?"

"I remember that night. I didn't put it together until recently. I didn't find out what I am until recently."

Callie straightens her shoulders like she's summoning courage. "His family live up in the deep woods. I could take you to see them if you want."

Charlie shakes his head. "No, I'm good. Maybe someday. For now, it's enough to have you." He looks over at me. "You and Annabel are all the family I need."

I smile at him through trembling lips, still marveling that I've become someone important to my lone wolf.

His mother turns and smiles at me, too. "You're braver than I was. You've accepted what he is. Thank you for loving my son."

I touch the bite marks again. "I wouldn't have him any other way."

AUTHOR'S NOTE

A huge thank you to the people who make this series possible: Aubrey Cara, for nipple-tassel wearing excellence and beta reads and Sandy Ebel of Personal Touch Editing. Lee Savino Goddesses and Renee's Romper Roomies—you bring us such joy!

And of course everyone who's read and reviewed the series thus far. We appreciate you! We'll have Trey's book for ya next. :)

XOXO

Renee & Lee

ALPHA'S TEMPTATION (BAD BOY ALPHAS, BOOK 1)

Read now

MINE TO PROTECT. MINE TO PUNISH. *MINE*.

I'm a lone wolf, and I like it that way. Banished from my birth pack after a bloodbath, I never wanted a mate.

Then I meet Kylie. *My temptation.* We're trapped in an elevator together, and her panic almost makes her pass out in my arms. She's strong, but broken. And she's hiding something.

My wolf wants to claim her. But she's human, and her delicate flesh won't survive a wolf's mark.

I'm too dangerous. I should stay away. But when I discover she's the hacker who nearly took down my company, I demand she submit to my punishment. And she will.

Kylie belongs to me.

ALPHA'S DANGER (BAD BOY ALPHAS, BOOK 2)

"YOU BROKE THE RULES, LITTLE HUMAN. I OWN YOU NOW."

I am an alpha wolf, one of the youngest in the States. I can pick any she-wolf in the pack for a mate. So why am I sniffing around the sexy human attorney next door? The minute I catch Amber's sweet scent, my wolf wants to claim her.

Hanging around is a bad idea, but I don't play by the rules. Amber acts all prim and proper, but she has a secret, too. She may not want her psychic abilities, but they're a gift.

I should let her go, but the way she fights me only makes me want her more. When she learns what I am, there's no escape for her. She's in my world, whether she likes it or not. I need her to use her gifts to help recover my missing sister —and I won't take no for an answer.

She's mine now.

READ NOW

ALPHA'S PRIZE (BAD BOY ALPHAS, BOOK 3)

MY CAPTIVE. MY MATE. MY PRIZE.

I didn't order the capture of the beautiful American she-wolf. I didn't buy her from the traffickers. I didn't even plan to claim her. But no male shifter could have withstood the test of a full moon and a locked room with Sedona, naked and shackled to the bed.

I lost control, not only claiming her, but also marking her, and leaving her pregnant with my wolfpup. I won't keep her prisoner, as much as I'd like to. I allow her to escape to the safety of her brother's pack.

But once marked, no she-wolf is ever really free. I will follow her to the ends of the Earth, if I must.

Sedona belongs to me.

Read Now

ALPHA'S CHALLENGE (BAD BOY ALPHAS, BOOK 4)

HOW TO DATE A WEREWOLF:

#1 Never call him 'Good Doggie.'

I've got a problem. A big, hairy problem. An enforcer from the Werewolves Motorcycle Club broke into my house. He thinks I know the Werewolves' secret, and the pack sent him to guard me.

#2 During a full moon, be ready to get freaky

By the time he decides I'm no threat, it's too late. His wolf has claimed me for his mate.

Too bad we can't stand each other...

 # 3 Bad girls get eaten in the bedroom

...until instincts take over. Things get wild. Naked under the full moon, this wolfman has me howling for more.

4 Break ups are hairy

Not even a visit from the mob, my abusive ex, my crazy mother and a road trip across the state in a hippie VW bus can shake him.

#5 Beware the mating bite

Because there's no running from a wolf when he decides you're his mate.

Read Now

ALPHA'S OBSESSION (BAD BOY ALPHA'S BOOK 5)

A werewolf, an owl shifter, and a scientist walk into a bar...

Sam

I was born in a lab, fostered out to humans, then tortured in a cage. Fate allowed me to escape, and I know why.

To balance the scales of justice. Right the misdeeds of the harvesters.

Nothing matters but taking down the man who made me what I am: A monster driven by revenge, whatever the cost.

Then I meet Layne. She thinks I'm a hero.

But she doesn't understand—If I don't follow this darkness to its end, it will consume me.

Layne

I've spent my life in the lab, researching the cure for the disease that killed my mom. No late nights out, no dates, definitely no boyfriend.

Then Sam breaks into my lab, steals my research, and

kidnaps me. He's damaged. Crazy. And definitely not human.

He and his friends are on a mission to stop the company that's been torturing shifters, and now I'm a part of it.

Sam promises to protect me. And when he touches me, I feel reborn. But he's hellbent on revenge. He won't give it up.

Not even for me.

Read Now

ALPHA'S DESIRE (BAD BOY ALPHA'S BOOK 6)

She's the one girl this player can't have. A human.

I'm dying to claim the redhead who lights up the club every Saturday night.

I want to pull her into the storeroom and make her scream, but it wouldn't be right.

She's too pure. Too fresh. Too passionate.

Too *human*.

When she learns my secret, my alpha orders me to wipe her memories.

But I won't do it.

Still, I'm not mate material—I can't mark her and bring her into the pack.

What in the hell am I going to do with her?

Read Now

ALPHA'S WAR (BAD BOY ALPHA'S BOOK 7)

I marked you. You belong to me.

Nash

I've survived suicide missions in war zones. Shifter prison labs. The worst torture imaginable. Nothing knocked me off my feet... until the beautiful lioness they threw in my cage. We shared one night before our captors ripped us apart.

Now I'm free, and my lion is going insane. He'll destroy me from the inside out if I don't find my mate.

I don't know who she is. I don't know where she lives. All I have is a video of her. But I'll die if I don't find her, and make her mine.

I'm coming for you, Denali.

Denali

They took me from my home, they killed my pride, they locked me up and forced me to breed. They took everything from me and still I survived.

But one night with a lion shifter destroyed me. Nash took the one thing my captors couldn't touch—my heart.

Somehow I escaped, and live in fear that they will come for me. It's killing my lioness, but I've got to hide—even from Nash. I've got to protect the one thing I have left to lose.

Our cub.

Read Now

ABOUT RENEE ROSE

USA TODAY BESTSELLING AUTHOR RENEE ROSE is a naughty wordsmith who writes kinky romance novels. Named Eroticon USA's Next Top Erotic Author in 2013, she has also won *The Romance Reviews* Best Historical Romance, and *Spanking Romance Reviews'* Best Historical, Best Erotic, Best Ageplay and favorite author. She's hit #1 on Amazon in the Erotic Paranormal, Western and Sci-fi categories. She also pens BDSM stories under the name Darling Adams.

Renee loves to connect with readers! Please visit her on:
Facebook | | Bookbub | Goodreads | Amazon | Instagram Blog | Twitter

KING OF DIAMONDS - A DARK MAFIA ROMANCE EXCERPT

I grab the vacuum and head back into the bedroom. When I finish, I hear male voices in the living room.

"Hope you can get some sleep, Nico. How long's it been?" one of the voices asked.

"Forty-eight hours. Fucking insomnia."

"G'luck, see you later." A door clicks shut.

My heart immediately beats a little faster with excitement or nerves. Yes—I'm a fool. Later, I would realize my mistake in not marching right out and introducing myself, but Marissa has me nervous about the Tacones and I freeze up. The cart stands out in the living room, though. I decide to go into the bathroom and clean everything I can without getting fresh supplies. Finally, I give up, square my shoulders and head out.

I arrive in the living room and pull out three folded towels, four hand towels and four washcloths. Out of my peripheral vision, I watch the broad shoulders and back of another finely dressed man.

He glances over then does a double-take. His dark eyes

rake over me, lingering on my legs and traveling up to my breasts, then face. "*Who the fuck are you?*"

I should've expected that response, but it startles me anyway. He sounds scary. Seriously scary, and he walks toward me like he means business. He's beautiful, with dark wavy hair, a stubbled square jaw and thick-lashed eyes that bore a hole right through me.

"Huh? Who. The fuck. Are you?"

I panic. Instead of answering him, I turn and walk swiftly to the bathroom, as if putting fresh towels in his bathroom will fix everything.

He stalks after me and follows me in. "What are you doing in here?" He knocks the towels out of my hands.

Stunned, I stare down at them scattered on the floor. "I'm...housekeeping," I offer lamely. Damn my idiotic fascination with the mafia. This is not the freaking *Sopranos*. This is a real-life, dangerous man wearing a gun in a holster under his armpit. I know, because I see it when he reaches for me.

He grips my upper arms. "Bullshit. No one who looks like"—his eyes travel up and down the length of my body again—"*you*—works in housekeeping."

I blink, not sure what that means. I'm pretty, I know that, but there's nothing special about me. I'm your girl-next-door blue-eyed blonde type, on the short and curvy side. Not like my cousin Corey, who is tall, slender, red-haired and drop-dead gorgeous, with the confidence to match.

There's something lewd in the way he looks at me that makes it sound like I'm standing there in nipple tassels and a G-string instead of my short, fitted maid's dress. I play dumb. "I'm new. I've only been here a couple weeks."

He sports dark circles under his eyes, and I remember

what he told the other man. He suffers from insomnia. Hasn't slept in forty-eight hours.

"Are you bugging the place?" he demands.

"Wha—" I can't even answer. I just stare like an idiot.

He starts frisking me for a weapon. "Is this a con? What do they think—I'm going to fuck you? Who sent you?"

I attempt to answer, but his warm hands sliding all over me make me forget what I was going to say. *Why is he talking about fucking me?*

He stands up and gives me a tiny shake. "Who. Sent. You?" His dark eyes mesmerize. He smells of the casino—of whiskey and cash, and beneath it, his own simmering essence.

"No one...I mean, Marissa!" I exclaim her name like a secret password, but it only seems to irritate him further.

He reaches out and runs his fingers swiftly along the collar of my housekeeping dress, as if checking for some hidden wiretap. I'm pretty sure the guy's half out of his mind, maybe delirious with sleep deprivation. Maybe just nuts. I freeze, not wanting to set him off.

To my shock, he yanks down the zipper on the front of my dress, all the way to my waist.

If I were my cousin Corey, daughter of a mean FBI agent, I'd knee him in the balls, gun or not. But I was raised not to make waves. To be a nice girl and do what authority tells me to do.

So, like a freaking idiot, I just stand there. A tiny mewl leaves my lips, but I don't dare move, don't protest. He yanks the form-fitting dress to my waist and jerks it down over my hips.

I wrest my arms free from the fabric to wrap them around myself.

Nico Tacone shoves me aside to get the dress out from

under my feet. He picks it up and runs his hands all over it, still searching for the mythical wiretap while I shiver in my bra and panties.

I fold my arms across my breasts. "Look, I'm not wearing a wire or bugging the place," I breathe. "I was helping Marissa and then she got a call—"

"Save it," he barks. "You're too fucking perfect. What's the con? What the fuck are you doing in here?"

I'm confounded. Should I keep arguing the truth when it only pisses him off? I swallow. None of the words in my head seem like the right ones to say.

He reaches for my bra.

I bat at his hands, heart pumping like I just did two back-to-back spin classes. He ignores my feeble resistance. The bra is a front hook and he obviously excels at removing women's lingerie because it's off faster than the dress. My breasts spring out with a bounce, and he glares at them, as if I bared them just to tempt him. He examines the bra, then tosses it on the floor and stares at me. His eyes dip once more to my breasts and his expression grows even more furious. "Real tits," he mutters as if that's a punishable offense.

I try to step back but I bump into the toilet. "I'm not hiding anything. I'm just a maid. I got hired two weeks ago. You can call Samuel."

He steps closer. Tragically, the hardened menace on his handsome face only increases his attractiveness to me. I really am wired wrong. My body thrills at the nearness of him, pussy dampening. Or maybe it's the fact that he just stripped me practically naked while he stands there fully clothed. I think this is a fetish to some people. Apparently, I'm one of them. If I wasn't so scared, it would be uber hot.

He palms my backside, warm fingers sliding over the

satiny fabric of my panties, but he's not groping me, he's still working efficiently, checking for bugs. He slides a thumb under the gusset, running the fabric through his fingers. My belly flutters.

Oh God. The back of his thumb brushes my dewy slit. I cringe in embarrassment. His head jerks up and he stares at me in surprise, nostrils flaring.

Then his brows slammed down as if it pisses him off I'm turned on, as if it's a trick.

That's when things really go to shit.

He pulls out his gun and points it at my head—actually pushes the cold hard muzzle against my brow. "*What. The fuck. Are you doing here?*"

KING OF DIAMONDS - A DARK MAFIA ROMANCE

Vegas Underground, Book One

I WARNED YOU.

I told you not to set foot in my casino again. I told you to stay away. Because if I see those hips swinging around my suite, I'll pin you against the wall and take you hard. And once I make you mine, I'm not gonna set you free.

Because I'm king of the Vegas underground and I take what I want.

So run. Stay the hell away from my casino.

Or I'll tie you to my bed. Put you on your knees.
    Break you.

Or else come to me, beautiful...

READ NOW

WANT FREE RENEE ROSE BOOKS?

Go to http://www.owned.gr8.com to sign up for Renee Rose's newsletter and receive a free copy of *Theirs to Protect, Owned by the Marine*, *Theirs to Punish, The Alpha's Punishment, Disobedience at the Dressmaker's* and *Her Billionaire Boss*. In addition to the free stories, you will also get special pricing, exclusive previews and news of new releases.

ALSO BY RENEE ROSE

Deathless Love
Deathless Discipline

The Winter Storm: An Ever After Chronicle

SCI-FI
Zandian Masters Series
His Human Slave
His Human Prisoner
Training His Human
His Human Rebel
His Human Vessel
His Mate and Master
Zandian Pet
Night of the Zandians
Bought by the Zandians

The Hand of Vengeance
Her Alien Masters

DARK MAFIA ROMANCE
King of Diamonds
The Russian, The Don's Daughter, Mob Mistress, The Bossman

CONTEMPORARY
Her Royal Master (Royally Mine)
The Russian
Black Light: Valentine Roulette
Theirs to Protect
Scoring with Santa
Owned by the Marine

BDSM under the name Darling Adams

ABOUT LEE SAVINO

Lee Savino is a USA today bestselling author, mom and choco-holic.

Warning: Do not read her Berserker series, or you will be addicted to the huge, dominant warriors who will stop at nothing to claim their mates.

I repeat: Do. Not. Read. The Berserker Saga. Particularly not the thrilling excerpt below.

Download a free book from www.leesavino.com (don't read that, either. Too much hot sexy lovin').

EXCERPT: SOLD TO THE BERSERKERS

A MÉNAGE SHIFTER ROMANCE

By Lee Savino

The day my stepfather sold me to the Berserkers, I woke at dawn with him leering over me. "Get up." He made to kick me and I scrambled out of my sleep stupor to my feet.

"I need your help with a delivery."

I nodded and glanced at my sleeping mother and siblings. I didn't trust my stepfather around my three younger sisters, but if I was gone with him all day, they'd be safe. I'd taken to carrying a dirk myself. I did not dare kill him; we needed him for food and shelter, but if he attacked me again, I would fight.

My mother's second husband hated me, ever since the last time he'd tried to take me and I had fought back. My mother was gone to market, and when he tried to grab me, something in me snapped. I would not let him touch me again. I fought, kicking and scratching, and finally grabbing an iron pot and scalding him with heated water.

He bellowed and looked as if he wanted to hurt me, but kept his distance. When my mother returned he pretended like nothing was wrong, but his eyes followed me with hatred and cunning.

Out loud he called me ugly and mocking the scar that marred my neck since a wild dog attacked me when I was young. I ignored this and kept my distance. I'd heard the taunts about my hideous face since the wounds had healed into scars, a mass of silver tissue at my neck.

That morning, I wrapped a scarf over my hair and scarred neck and followed my stepfather, carrying his wares down the old road. At first I thought we were headed to the great market, but when we reached the fork in the road and he went an unfamiliar way, I hesitated. Something wasn't right.

"This way, cur." He'd taken to calling me "dog". He'd taunted me, saying the only sounds I could make were grunts like a beast, so I might as well be one. He was right. The attack had taken my voice by damaging my throat.

If I followed him into the forest and he tried to kill me, I wouldn't even be able to cry out.

"There's a rich man who asked for his wares delivered to his door." He marched on without a backward glance and I followed.

I had lived all my life in the kingdom of Alba, but when my father died and my mother remarried, we moved to my stepfather's village in the highlands, at the foot of the great, forbidding mountains. There were stories of evil that lived in the dark crevices of the heights, but I'd never believed them.

I knew enough monsters living in plain sight.

The longer we walked, the lower the sun sank in the sky, the more I knew my stepfather was trying to trick me, that there was no rich man waiting for these wares.

When the path curved, and my stepfather stepped out

from behind a boulder to surprise me, I was half ready, but before I could reach for my dirk he struck me so hard I fell.

I woke tied to a tree.

The light was lower, heralding dusk. I struggled silently, frantic gasps escaping from my scarred throat. My stepfather stepped into view and I felt a second of relief at a familiar face, before remembering the evil this man had wrought on my body. Whatever he was planning, it would bode ill for me, and my younger sisters. If I didn't survive, they would eventually share the same fate as mine.

"You're awake," he said. "Just in time for the sale."

I strained but my bonds held fast. As my stepfather approached, I realized that the scarf that I wrapped around my neck to hide my scars had fallen, exposing them. Out of habit, I twitched my head to the side, tucking my bad side towards my shoulder.

My stepfather smirked.

"So ugly," he sneered. "I could never find a husband for you, but I found someone to take you. A group of warriors passing through who saw you, and want to slake their lust on your body. Who knows, if you please them, they may let you live. But I doubt you'll survive these men. They're foreigners, mercenaries, come to fight for the king. Berserkers. If you're lucky your death will be swift when they tear you apart."

I'd heard the tales of berserker warriors, fearsome warriors of old. Ageless, timeless, they'd sailed over the seas to the land, plundering, killing, taking slaves, they fought for our kings, and their own. Nothing could stand in their path when they went into a killing rage.

I fought to keep my fear off my face. Berserker's were a myth, so my stepfather had probably sold me to a band of passing soldiers who would take their pleasure from my flesh before leaving me for dead, or selling me on.

"I could've sold you long ago, if I stripped you bare and put a bag over you head to hide those scars."

His hands pawed at me, and I shied away from his disgusting breath. He slapped me, then tore at my braid, letting my hair spill over my face and shoulders.

Bound as I was, I still could glare at him. I could do nothing to stop the sale, but I hoped my fierce expression told him I'd fight to the death if he tried to force himself on me.

His hand started to wander down towards my breast when a shadow moved on the edge of the clearing. It caught my eye and I startled. My stepfather stepped back as the warriors poured from the trees.

My first thought was that they were not men, but beasts. They prowled forward, dark shapes almost one with the shadows. A few wore animal pelts and held back, lurking on the edge of the woods. Two came forward, wearing the garb of warriors, bristling with weapons. One had dark hair, and the other long, dirty blond with a beard to match.

Their eyes glowed with a terrifying light.

As they approached, the smell of raw meat and blood wafted over us, and my stomach twisted. I was glad my stepfather hadn't fed me all day, or I would've emptied my guts on the ground.

My stepfather's face and tone took on the wheedling expression I'd seen when he was selling in the market.

"Good evening, sirs," he cringed before the largest, the blond with hair streaming down his chest.

They were perfectly silent, but the blond approached, fixing me with strange golden eyes.

Their faces were fair enough, but their hulking forms

and the quick, light way they moved made me catch my breath. I had never seen such massive men. Beside them, my stepfather looked like an ugly dwarf.

"This is the one you wanted," my stepfather continued. "She's healthy and strong. She will be a good slave for you."

My body would've shaken with terror, if I were not bound so tightly.

A dark haired warrior stepped up beside the blond and the two exchanged a look.

"You asked for the one with scars." My stepfather took my hair and jerked my head back, exposing the horrible, silvery mass. I shut my eyes, tears squeezing out at the sudden pain and humiliation.

The next thing I knew, my stepfather's grip loosened. A grunt, and I opened my eyes to see the dark haired warrior standing at my side. My stepfather sprawled on the ground as if he'd been pushed.

The blond leader prodded a boot into my stepfather's side.

"Get up," the blond said, in a voice that was more a growl than a human sound. It curdled my blood. My stepfather scrambled to his feet.

The black haired man cut away the last of my bonds, and I sagged forward. I would've fallen but he caught me easily and set me on my feet, keeping his arms around me. I was not the smallest woman, but he was a giant. Muscles bulged in his arms and chest, but he held me carefully. I stared at him, taking in his raven dark hair and strange gold eyes.

He tucked me closer to his muscled body.

Meanwhile, my stepfather whined. "I just wanted to show you the scars—"

Again that frightening growl from the blond. "You don't touch what is ours."

"I don't want to touch her." My stepfather spat.

Despite myself, I cowered against the man who held me. A stranger I had never met, he was still a safer haven than my stepfather.

"I only wish to make sure you are satisfied, milords. Do you want to sample her?" my stepfather asked in an evil tone. He wanted to see me torn apart.

A growl rumbled under my ear and I lifted my head. Who were these men, these great warriors who had bought and paid for me? The arms around my body were strong and solid, inescapable, but the gold eyes looking down at me were kind. The warrior ran his thumb across the pad of my lips, and his fingers were gentle for such a large, violent looking warrior. Under the scent of blood, he smelled of snow and sharp cold, a clean scent.

He pressed his face against my head, breathing in a deep breath.

The blond was looking at us.

"It's her," the black haired man growled, his voice so guttural. "This is the one."

One of his hands came to cover the side of my face and throat, holding my face to his chest in a protective gesture.

I closed my eyes, relaxing in the solid warmth of the warrior's body.

A clink of gold, and the deed was done. I'd been sold.

Almost immediately, the warrior started pulling me away.

I fought my rising panic, wishing that my stepfather's was not the last familiar face I saw.

"Goodbye, Brenna," my stepfather smirked as the warriors streamed past him, following their blond leader into the forest.

"Wait," the blond stopped. Immediately the warriors grabbed my stepfather. "Her name is Brenna?"

"Yes. But you bought her. Call her what you like."

The dark haired warrior tugged me on. I half followed, half staggered along beside him. My nails bit into my palms so I could keep myself from panicking. Fighting the giant beside me wasn't an option. Neither was trying to outrun him.

The blond joined us, and the two warriors pulled me into the dark grove. Terrible thoughts poured into my mind. I belonged to these men, and now they would rape me, sate themselves with my body, then cut my throat and leave me for the wolves.

My eyes filled with tears, both angry and frightened.

They stopped as one and drew me between them. I shut my eyes in defiance, and the tears leaked out.

As I healed from the attack, I could make some noises, horrible, animal things, but they were so ugly, I stopped making any sounds at all. Sometimes, when alone, I'd sink into the river, open my mouth and try to scream. But no sound came out anymore. My throat had forgotten my voice.

Now the only sound in the grove was my harsh breathing.

I sensed the warriors on either side of me, their massive shapes towering over my fragile body. I was much smaller than them, tiny and petite beside their massive forms.

Right now I tried to remember to breathe and submit to these men. One blow and they could kill me.

My heart beat so hard it was painful. I was ready to die.

But when they touched me they were gentle. A hand

brushed back my hair, then stroked my jaw. One steadied me from behind as the other cupped my head and turned my head this way and that. The one behind me gathered my hair behind me. I held my breath as the two massive warriors handled me.

I realized the smell of blood had fallen away, replaced by another scent, an animal musk that was much more pleasant.

A finger ran over my neck, near the scar and I sucked in a breath. The hands dropped away.

Their faces dipped close to mine, and I felt their breath on my skin as if they took deep scents of my hair.

"So good," one of them groaned.

I didn't understand. I was afraid of them taking me but I didn't know why they weren't.

"It's working," one murmured to the other. "The witch was right."

As they dipped their heads and scented me, my heart beat faster in response to their proximity. Something stirred deep inside me. Desire. A few minutes alone with these men and I'd been more intimate with them than any other.

As one they bent their heads to mine, nuzzling close to my neck a tingling spread over my skin.

I felt it then, unbidden, a stirring in my loins. Ever since I had come into womanhood, my desires were strong. Every month I fought the pull to find a man and join with him. I was hideous and destined to be an outcast and alone. But each full moon my body came alive, beset by waves of roiling lust until I felt desperate enough to grab the nearest man and beg him to give me sons.

The heat poured over me until I heard a gasp—one of the warriors jerked back and stepped away.

"She's ready," one growled. Instead of frightening, the sound excited me.

What was happening?

"Not here, brother," the blond rasped.

Without answering, the dark-haired one pulled me on.

For a while we walked, pushing through the forest and forded a stream. The heat in me faded as I followed, weak with hunger and fear, eventually stumbling on exhaustion numbed feet.

The dark-haired warrior stopped, and I flinched, expecting him to bully me into continuing on.

Instead, he guided me to face him. Again his hands came to me, stroking back my hair. I winced when I realized what he was doing: looking at my scar.

Involuntarily my head jerked and he let my chin go, offering me water instead. He held the skin while I drank, and when I'd had my fill he offered me dried meat, feeding me from his hand. I stared into the strange golden eyes, unable to keep the questions off my face: Who are you? What are you going to do with me?

When I was done, he lay a hand on his chest and uttered a guttural sound I didn't understand. He repeated it twice, then lay his hand on my chest.

"Brenna." I could barely make out my name, but I nodded.

A shadow of a smile curved his full lips. Shrugging off the gray pelt he wore, he wrapped it around my shoulders before pulling me back into the circle of his strong arms.

My heart beat faster. The pelt's warmth seeped into my tired body, and the big man held me steady. I still felt frightened, but waited obediently in the dark haired warrior's embrace. I dared not struggle.

The brush around us rippled and the warriors

surrounded us. I shrank towards my black-haired captor, but he held me fast, turning me so I faced the warrior who seemed to be their leader.

The blond was so huge, my neck had to tip back to see him. He moved forward and I couldn't help trembling so hard I would've fallen if the dark haired warrior let me go. Every instinct in me screamed that this was a wild man, a beast a dangerous monster and I needed to run.

He reached out and I flinched.

His hand halted.

He swallowed, as if trying to remember how to use his voice.

"Brenna." My name was no more than a soft growl. "We mean you no harm."

I studied him. As big as the warriors were, the blond was one of the largest. He walked lightly, muscles bulging. Long locks of blond hair brushed his broad shoulders. His face was rawboned and half covered in a beard, the defining feature his great gold eyebrows over those amazing eyes.

When his gaze caught mine, his eyes glowed.

His hands touched my face, a thumb stroking my lips. He tilted it to and fro. He pushed my hair away from my neck. I shut my eyes, knowing what he saw, the white weals and gnarled tissue, healed into a disfiguring scar that had taken my voice, and nearly taken my life.

I barely remembered the attack: a large dark shape rushing at me from the shadows, then pain. Lots of pain. My mother told me I lay near death for days. No one thought I would survive, but I did.

Some believed it would be better if I hadn't. Even though I healed from the attack, the scars marked my face and my life. The boys used to chase me down the street, throwing things. I grew up learning to blend into the shadows. To move silently so I wouldn't draw attention to myself. Later, when my mother married my stepfather, I learned to cower and hide.

Her body is pretty enough, my stepfather had said. *Just put a bag over her head so you can stand it.*

Now my new owner tipped my head this way and that, studying the scar. He nodded, looking satisfied. "The mark of the wolf," he rasped.

A ripple went around the assembled men, and the other warriors pressed closer. The black haired man held me still, hefty arms around my body.

I wished I could ask what the blond warrior meant.

The men surrounded me, staring at my hideous scars.

My blond captor released my jaw and I ducked my head down again in shame. His large, rough hands caught my head again, and raised it, but this time he cupped my face.

I shut my eyes. I couldn't even cry out. This man now owned me. I'd resigned myself to living life with a disfigured face, unwanted and unloved, but I'd never thought I'd become a slave.

"Brenna," The command came in that rasping growl. "Look at me."

Somehow I obeyed and met the leader's steady gaze. Something in that golden glow mesmerized me, and I felt calmer.

"Do not be afraid." His throat worked for a moment, as if he was trying to remember how to speak. "Is it true you cannot speak?"

I nodded.

"Can you read or write?"

I shook my head. This was the strangest conversation I'd had in my nineteen years.

He looked frustrated, exchanging glances with the warrior who held me.

A voice spoke at my ear, still rough and guttural, but a bit more clearly than before. "We would like to find a way to talk to ye." The speaker turned me to face him, and I flinched as he brought his hand up, but he only examined the scars as the blond had.

By the time he was done, all warriors but the blond had melted away. Dark hair touched my cheek and I winced, realizing there was a bruise on my face from when my step-father struck me.

The blond crowded closer, a sound rumbling in his great chest, not unlike a growl.

"Brenna," he said. "We will not hurt you. I swear it. No one will ever hurt you again."

The dark haired one took a few locks of my hair in his hand, gripping them lightly and raising them to his face. He breathed in my scent, then looked at me with glowing eyes and said in a clear voice.

"Ye belong to us now."

The rest of the night passed in a blur. We walked into the woods, the thick darkness, and went along a path. The warriors went behind and before, I was safe in the middle.

Finally exhaustion took over and I stumbled. Instantly, the dark haired warrior swung me up in his arms, and the group's pace increased. His hand came up, pressing my face to his neck.

I must have slept, for when I woke again, the blond was carrying me. I lifted my head blinking in the starlight and cold night air. The warriors must have walked all night, and were still hiking, following a trail up a mountain. I roused a little and stared into the leaders golden eyes.

"Sleep," he grunted. "Almost home."

I do not know how long I slept, but as I slept I dreamed. The starlight fell away into a deeper darkness. I was in a warm, safe place with two warriors leaning over me, large hands sifting through my hair. One of them pulled out a dirk and sliced away my gown, and then the hands began stroking down my body. Their touches fed my heated desire, and in my dream I longed to pull their bodies over mine, wordlessly begging them to fill me.

Instead, I lay still as they touched me with reverent fingers. I heard them speak, but not out loud. They didn't use words but somehow I understood them.

"The witch was right. She calms the wolf."

A grunt of agreement, then a pause. "I can smell her heat."

"Patience, brother. We have waited this long."

They lay on either side of me, still touching me. In the darkness their eyes glowed.

"Brother," one said in a tone of awe. "The beast rests."

"As does mine."

"It has been so long."

"Too long. But the struggle is over. The beast will sleep again."

SOLD TO THE BERSERKERS

When Brenna's father sells her to a band of passing warriors, her only thought is to survive. She doesn't expect to be claimed by the two fearsome warriors who lead the Berserker clan. Kept in captivity, she is coddled and cared for, treated more like a savior than a slave. Can captivity lead to love? And when she discovers the truth behind the myth of the fearsome warriors, can she accept her place as the Berserkers' true mate?

∾

Author's Note: *Sold to the Berserkers is a standalone, short, MFM ménage romance starring two huge, dominant warriors who make it all about the woman. Read the whole best-selling Berserker saga to see what readers are raving about...*

The Berserker Saga

Bred by the Berserkers (free novella available on leesavino.com)

Taken by the Berserkers

Given to the Berserkers

Claimed by the Berserkers

Rescued by the Berserkers - free on all sites, including Wattpad

Captured by the Berserkers

Kidnapped by the Berserkers

Bonded to the Berserkers

Berserker Babies

Owned by the Berserkers

Night of the Berserkers

ALSO BY LEE SAVINO

The Berserker Saga

Sold to the Berserkers

Mated to the Berserkers

Bred by the Berserkers (FREE novella only available at www.leesavino.com)

Taken by the Berserkers

Given to the Berserkers

Claimed by the Berserkers

Berserker Brides

Rescued by the Berserker - FREE on all ebook platforms!

Captured by the Berserkers

Kidnapped by the Berserkers

Bonded to the Berserkers

Owned by the Berserkers

Mastered by the Berserkers - coming soon

Tamed by the Berserkers - coming soon

Protected by the Berserkers - coming soon

Trained by the Berserkers - coming soon

Night of the Berserkers

Berserker Babies

Draekons (Dragons in Exile) with Lili Zander

Bad Boy Alphas with Renee Rose

Contemporary Romance

Her Marine Daddy

Printed in Great Britain
by Amazon

20381755R00132